Sheffield
City Council

Renew this item at:
http://library.sheffield.gov.uk
or contact your local library

LIBRARIES, ARCHIVES & INFORMATION

INPECTOR WEST SERIES

Inspector West Takes Charge

Inspector West Leaves Town (Also published as: Go Away to Murder)

Inspector West at Home (Also published as: An Apostle of Gloom)

Inspector West Regrets

Holiday for Inspector West

Battle for Inspector West

Triumph for Inspector West (Also published as: The Case Against Paul Raeburn)

Inspector West Kicks Off (Also published as: Sport for Inspector West)

Inspector West Alone

Inspector West Cries Wolf (Also published as: The Creepers)

A Case for Inspector West (Also published as: The Figure in the Dusk)

Puzzle for Inspector West (Also published as: The Dissemblers)

Inspector West at Bay (Also published as: The Case of the Acid Throwers)

A Gun for Inspector West (Also published as: Give a Man a Gun)

Send Inspector West (Also published as: Send Superintendent West)

A Beauty for Inspector West (Also published as: The Beauty Queen Killer)

Inspector West Makes Haste (Also published as: Murder Makes Haste)

Two for Inspector West (Also published as: Murder: One, Two, Three)

Parcels for Inspector West (Also published as: Death of a Postman)

A Prince for Inspector West (Also published as: Death of a Assassin)

Accident for Inspector West (Also published as: Hit and Run)

Find Inspector West (Also published as: Doorway to Death)

Murder, London - New York

Strike for Death (Also published as: The Killing Strike)

Death of a Racehorse

The Case of the Innocent Victims

Murder on the Line

Death in Cold Print

The Scene of the Crime

Policeman's Dread

Hang the Little Man

Look Three Ways at Murder

Murder, London - Australia

Murder, London - South Africa

The Executioners

So Young to Burn

Murder, London - Miami

A Part for a Policeman

Alibi (Also published as: Alibi for Inspector West)

A Splinter of Glass

The Theft of Magna Carta

The Extortioners

A Sharp Rise in Crime

Battle for
Inspector West

John Creasey

HOUSE OF
STRATUS

This edition published in 204 by House of Stratus, an imprint of Stratus Books Ltd., Lisandra House, Fore Street, Looe, Cornwall, PL13 1AD, U.K. www.houseofstratus.com

Typeset by House of Stratus.

A catalogue record for this book is available from the British Library and the Library of Congress.

ISBN 07551-2343-3
EAN 978-07551-2343-8

Chapter One

Wedding March

The bride, a radiant vision in white, had gone into St Margaret's, and her bridesmaids had disappeared after her; all that remained visible was the crowd of sightseers.

A man stood near the door of the church, his eyes lowered, his expression humble. He was poorly but neatly dressed. His head was bare now, although he had worn a hat, pulled low over his eyes, when the bride and bridegroom and their party had gone inside the church.

The man's face was thin and pale, his hair turning grey. He had wrinkles at his eyes and mouth.

Almost immediately opposite him, mixing with the crowd, was an upstanding man with squared shoulders in a neat brown suit. He had a large face with broad features and a pair of shrewd, penetrating eyes. Every now and again he glanced at the grey-haired man, only to look away as soon as the other glanced towards him.

He was Detective-Sergeant Jameson, of Scotland Yard, and he was puzzled. Then his face cleared suddenly. He looked away from the humble man, and caught the eye of a Detective-Officer who stood in the crowd on the other side of the path.

The DO read the message in Jameson's eyes, pushed his way through the crowd, and joined him. Two or three of the old-stagers in this game of watching weddings nudged one another, recognising

1

these men as detectives. But no one heard what Jameson said except the DO.

'That little chap, at the front, Peel—see him?'

'Yes,' said Peel, who was also large and tall and broad-featured; the two might have been brothers.

'That's Arthur Morely,' Jameson whispered. 'I just remember him. Sentenced to death for the murder of his wife twelve or thirteen years ago. Sentence commuted—he's only been out a month or two. Keep an eye on him.'

'Wonder what he's doing here?' said Peel.

Jameson said dryly: 'Wouldn't you like to see your own daughter married?'

Now the first notes of Mendelssohn's 'Wedding March' came from the church, there was a stir among the crowd, and the man whom Jameson had recognised put on his hat and pulled it low over his eyes. Jameson, who was always on the look-out for trouble, thought that none was really likely here; if Morely were planning to make a scene, he wouldn't hide his face. It wasn't surprising that he did not want to be recognised. He looked a nice, old chap, although 'old' was hardly justified; Morely wasn't yet fifty.

Jameson remembered a little about the circumstances of the murder. There had been a quarrel over another man, and Morely had strangled his wife. The trial had been quite short; there had hardly been any defence, except that of extreme provocation. And the prosecution had proved beyond all reasonable doubt that Morely's wife had never had a lover; that the man's jealousy had been unreasoning and unjustified.

A rustle of interest ran through the crowd, as bride and bridegroom appeared. Cameras clicked. Jameson, trying to see everything at once, caught a glimpse of Christine Morely's face – Christine Grant now – and saw a mingling of beauty, excitement and radiance; he had seldom seen a woman look so happy.

Michael Grant's smile faded when he saw the photographer, but it quickly returned.

He was a tall, slim, striking-looking man; the son of a famous father, and in spite of that overshadowing personality he had made a reputation for himself. Eton, Oxford, Big Business, the RAF, test pilot, Big Business again; that summed up Michael Grant's career. He was in the middle-thirties, ten or twelve years older than his wife.

Morely, standing quite still, moved his hat from his forehead as the couple passed, and watched his daughter until she reached the Daimler limousine which had now pulled up. She stepped inside. Morely sighed, and turned away.

Even now, it wasn't over. A little crowd of friends gathered round the Rolls Bentley in which the Grants were to travel on the first stage of their honeymoon. They were to spend a week or two in Devon and then go to the Riviera. The first was for sentimental reasons: they had met in Devon, where Sir Mortimer Grant had a beautiful old house, Tivern Lodge. The newly-weds were going there immediately after the ceremony; Michael Grant's manservant, Haydon, had left for Devon with most of the luggage.

Still radiant, Christine made her way laughingly to the car, dressed now in a bottle-green suit by Dior. Grant climbed in beside her, and the car moved off.

Christine brushed the confetti from her shoulders and lap, then from Michael's. He glanced at her, smiling, but kept his eyes on the thick traffic ahead.

When they were on the Great West Road, Grant relaxed, and caught Christine's eye.

'All well, sweet?'

'All's wonderful!' She had never meant a thing more.

'I hope to God I always make you feel like that.'

'Darling, you will! Where are we staying tonight?'

'You'll find out,' said Grant, solemnly.

'You're not going to try to reach Tivern, are you?'

'I am only a fool sometimes, and this isn't jet-propelled. I've selected a delightful little spot,' he assured her. 'We'll be just in time to have a rest and, if you feel like it, change for dinner.'

'Somewhere in Dorset, then?'

'The hilly wilds of North Dorset,' Grant said lightly. 'Let's see if we can get a bit of speed on, shall we, the road's empty.'

Christine didn't care where they went, hardly knew what she was saying. She was in a daze of happiness, an I-must-touch-him-to-be-sure-he's-real mood. And it showed in her eyes.

'Nothing over a hundred, darling!'

Grant grinned at her.

The road here was flat, the land on either side uninteresting, but some way ahead were trees and, in the distance, undulating meadowland. After three minutes of exhilarating speed, Grant eased off the accelerator. By the time they reached a patch of beech trees which hid a corner, they were travelling at no more than forty.

He looked at her again; adoringly; newly-wed.

'Happy?'

'So happy.'

Then a car, a big green Mercedes, passed them on the bend.

Grant glared, for he abominated road-hogs and jay-walkers. Christine saw the corners of his lips turn down. As the other car shot ahead, a passenger in the back seat looked round, and Christine saw him clearly; a little man with a pale, round face – smiling a set smile, a Chinaman's smile.

The car disappeared round another corner.

Christine began: 'Why *will* people ask for trouble? I—'

She broke off.

It was as if a dark cloud had fallen over her husband's face. It was set in bleak lines, reminding her of granite, revealing the hard streak which she knew was there, although he had never shown it to her before. The other car was now a hundred yards ahead, travelling very fast. Christine could just make out the head and shoulders of the driver, but not of the passenger.

It was on the tip of her tongue to ask what had upset Michael, but she stopped herself. He'd tell her, in good time. It was crazy, but they were comparative strangers to each other, and had to learn about each other's moods, learn to dovetail their lives. She mustn't try to hurry it, must fit her mood into his; she owed him that; she felt that she worshipped him.

Then he turned to look at her and his expression was almost frightening, something she had never dreamt could show in him. He was *afraid*.

Grant looked at her as if he hardly knew she was sitting beside him. Then gradually his expression changed, his lips curved, and somehow his face became strong and free from fear. He took a hand off the wheel and squeezed her knee.

'We've made good time; how about a mystery-tour? Care to make a detour?'

'No! We *might* get a puncture or have some engine trouble, and I'd hate to spend our first night under a haystack.'

He gave a deep, amused chuckle.

'I don't know that I'd care,' he said, 'but you're probably right.'

The green Mercedes was out of sight, the road was good, and they were able to make fine speed. Grant seemed to have forgotten whatever had upset him, although Christine couldn't get it out of her mind. She hoped she did not show that.

They reached Salisbury two hours after leaving London, and beneath the archway of a sixteenth-century coaching inn, where ivy clustered at the walls, the windows still had bottle glass, and the oak beams were twisted and gnarled, as if still growing in the walls.

'Tea, Mrs Grant?'

'How on earth did you guess I was parched?'

He helped her out of the car, and under the patient eyes of an old porter, brushed a few pieces of confetti from her coat. Then, arm-in-arm, they went towards the back entrance of the hotel. The big lounge was half-empty, and pleasantly cool. A pleasant waitress in a black frock and tiny bonnet cap took their order. They talked idly, foolishly, gaily – and Christine almost forgot the green Mercedes too. But soon after they started off again, Christine felt that he was alert, wary.

They were only a mile or two out, nearing Wilton and still in a built-up district, when the green Mercedes passed them. Her heart missed a beat. But this time the car committed no offence against the Highway Code, and the passenger sat in a corner without looking round. Grant's expression did not change, but Christine saw that his hands tightened on the wheel.

Before long, they turned off the main road into a lane – and he gave her no warning. Then he swung the car off the lane into a little copse, and jolted to a standstill. He drew her towards him until her head was resting on his shoulder and brushed her forehead with his lips.

'Darling, I have a dark past,' he announced, with a kind of mock solemnity.

'I've no doubt about that!' He was going to explain, she felt, and it was a reward for waiting.

'This is not a confession,' he assured her, 'Just a statement of fact. May I be melodramatic?'

'*Can* you be?' A little uneasily Christine wondered what was coming.

'Oh, yes,' said Grant. 'I can be most melodramatic. None better, sweet. I must tell you the dark secret of my life. I have an *enemy*.'

'Oh!' cried Christine, and tried to enter into his mood. But her heart lurched. 'A mortal enemy?'

'One who would gladly stick his knife into my gizzard,' declaimed Grant, and although his manner was flippant, a spasm of fear shot through her, almost one of dread; but it was quickly gone. 'A man I wronged, or who imagined that I wronged him,' Grant went on, 'One who—'

He broke off and smiled.

'That's about the size of it, sweet! I thought the business with a man I once quarrelled with was all over, but I saw him on the road just now. It shook me, although it was probably coincidence.'

'The man with the Chinaman's smile?' asked Christine.

'I thought you'd noticed something, but I couldn't think you'd spotted him so quickly,' Grant said. 'The man with the Chinaman's smile—*very* apt.'

'Thank you, sir.'

'Oh, due praise where praise is due.' He was again completely at ease, smiling – trouble-free. 'It's a long story, sweet. You might almost call it a family feud. He lost a great deal of money, and swore vengeance, but as he left the country, I thought for good, his threat wasn't likely to make me lose any sleep. Now he's chosen today to show up, damn and blast him.'

'It can hardly be just coincidence,' said Christine, reluctantly.

'I take that back,' said Grant. 'More likely he wants to worry me on this day of great bliss. I'm glad I haven't kept it to myself.'

'So am I,' said Christine warmly. She wanted to ask a dozen questions, but decided again that it was wiser not to press him, he would explain in his own good time. She still tried to be flippant. 'We'll have to lock our door tonight.'

'He can't know where we're staying,' said Grant confidently, 'and this detour should make sure he isn't able to follow us. We won't touch the main road again for twenty miles.'

They drove through by-lanes for nearly an hour, sometimes silent, sometimes gay. Grant hadn't yet said where they were going, but after they had driven along the main road again for ten minutes, he said: 'We're there!'

Standing back from the road was a large, one-storeyed building, with a low, thatched roof, warm yellow-red bricks, and a garden which from here looked a picture of gay colours.

Grant pulled up outside the open front door.

'You get out, my sweet,' he said. 'I won't be a jiffy putting the car away.'

He leaned across her to open the door as a man wearing a short white coat came from the bungalow. He did not appear to hurry, but reached the car before the door opened.

'May I take your luggage, sir?'

'The two cases in the back, please.' Grant waited until the large suitcases had been taken out and Christine stood at the foot of a small flight of steps. 'Two minutes,' he said, and gave her a smile which was almost fierce as he drove off.

Christine looked over the valley and the hills beyond it, and for a few moments her thoughts were free of uncertainty and fears, but that ecstatic happiness had gone.

The bungalow was built on the side of the valley, and a great sweep of grassland on either side of the drive spread out. Christine waited, without looking into the hotel, until Grant returned, tossing his keys up in the air and catching them.

'Well?' he asked.

'Marvellous!'

Grant chuckled.

'I thought you'd like it. A country hotel which is more like a club. I came across it some years ago, and always wanted to come back. Care for a week or two here?'

'I'd love it.' She didn't say that she thought they were going to Tivern, or remind him that their main luggage had gone ahead of them, but it was not so easy to ignore his reticence.

The entrance hall was pleasant, with glass doors on either side leading to the main lounge and the dining-room. The walls were panelled in light oak, the furniture was modern and comfortable, the Axminster carpets were thick and yielding. Two or three people sat on a lawn opposite the front door, and farther away two girls were playing tennis, they could hear the whang of the ball on the rackets. The sun shone on water near the courts, and on a low pale blue and white building, on a diving platform and a fountain. Farther away, a little group of people on horseback were riding towards the bungalow.

Grant led the way along a wide passage, with doors at long intervals, and the porter came out of the end door on the right.

'If there is anything you need, sir, you'll let me know, won't you?'

'Yes, thanks.' Grant smiled and reached the door before Christine and flung it open. It was furnished with comfortable chairs, and had panelled walls, a shelf all round on which stood willow-pattern dishes, copper pots and pans, jugs and brasses.

'Now inspect the bridal chamber,' said Grant. 'Door in that corner leads to our bathroom. Armchairs to idle hours away, and just look at the view!'

'I have been,' said Christine. 'I—oh, darling, we're really here!'

They stood side by side, arms interlocked, looking out of the window, and a feeling of security and contentment spread over Christine, and with it a kind of breathless wonder that he had fallen in love with her.

'What time's dinner?' she asked abruptly. 'I'll unpack, then—'
'We'll share all chores,' Grant said firmly. 'Not that there's much to do.' He opened her case, and saw that it was packed to overflowing. 'Rather more than one dinner-dress,' he said dryly. 'Can I hang anything up?'

'I'll do the dresses,' she said, and crossed to the wardrobe, gay and light-hearted, and opened the door.

She screamed!

Grant sprang to her, and saw in a flash what had frightened her. Hanging inside the wardrobe was a face – a cardboard face, swinging gently from the movement of the door; the face of a grinning Chinaman.

Chapter Two

Pink Mr Prendergast

Christine, trembling helplessly, saw that the face was life-size, and so skilfully painted that at first glimpse it looked almost real. It was fastened by a loop of string to a clothes-hanger. Grant took it down. Closer inspection showed that it was not really a Chinaman's face, or even Oriental, but it had the set grin which they had seen on the face of the man in the Mercedes. Even a lock of dark hair, falling over the forehead, was there.

Grant put an arm about Christine's waist.

'I'm so sorry about this, darling. So terribly sorry, I thought this place was absolutely safe.'

Christine couldn't speak.

'At least I prepared you a little,' Grant said.

She moistened her lips.

'Yes, you did. I—I shall be all right in a minute.'

He pulled her towards him and gave her a hug which made her gasp.

'Now I *know* what a bear-hug is,' she said breathlessly, and tried to be bright, making herself remember that it would be folly to try to make him tell her more; his confidence must come freely. 'This is an awfully bad start to our married life, Mike.'

'It's damnable, I know, but—'

'I mean, you've made such an awful flop of arrangements,' Christine said hurriedly. 'I don't so much mind Chin-chin Chinaman, but to think that you made all these plans to prevent him from finding out where we'd be, yet he was here ahead of us. It's shocking bad staff-work.'

'Hum-hum-hum,' murmured Grant. 'Yes. If I weren't desperately in love with you already, I'd start right now.' How that did her heart good, another great reward for patience. 'You didn't tell me that you had nerves of iron and a pretty wit at times of crisis. Yes, I made plans which I thought were foolproof. Yes, I did know he was back. It was a question of letting Chin-chin put a spanner in the works and postponing the wedding until he was rendered harmless, or pretending that he didn't exist and hoping that he would have the sense to keep out of the limelight. It's only a week or two since I knew he was back in England, and you know what these gossips are. Imagine them whispering: *"And he practically left her at the church, m'dear."'* He gave a little bitter laugh. 'Can't you hear them?'

'Yes, I think I can. Mike, don't look like that! If there's a thing I'm quite sure about, it's your love for me. Of course, I wish you'd felt that you could have told me about this before, but—'

'But you wouldn't have had half so much fun a-trousseauing,' protested Grant, 'and you'd have been looking all about you in church and not listening to the parson, imagining some slant-eyed villain standing among the crowd outside, preparing to do violence.'

'I suppose you're right,' Christine conceded. It was good to think that he had kept this back for her sake, not his own.

'Let's try to forget it for a while,' said Grant. 'Eat, drink and be merry, for tomorrow we fly!'

So he wasn't going to explain any more yet.

'Fly where?'

'Almost anywhere,' said Grant. 'I'm determined to have an uninterrupted honeymoon,'

'Darling,' said Christine, pressing the bell with great deliberation, 'we are not going to run away. What kind of honeymoon would it be if we worried in case we were coming back to—well, to whatever this is? We're going to stay here until it's all over, then we'll have a guaranteed trouble-free honeymoon!' She looked up at a tap at the door. 'What I'd love is a drink, I'll feel better then.'

A white-coated lad came in, with oily, black hair and a sallow, unsmiling face.

'A gin-and-lime, a double-whisky and some soda-water,' Grant ordered.

'Yes, sir.' The lad went out.

'I wonder if you're right about staying,' Grant mused. 'Chin-chin might not stay in England very long, because he has a police record as long as that waiter's face.' Then how had the man come to know Michael? 'We might go away for two or three weeks, then come back to find that all is well. Let's dine on it, we'll talk more about it afterwards. How long will it take you to change?'

'About half an hour.'

'I only want ten minutes,' said Grant. 'When we've had our drinks, I'll take a look round the hotel grounds and see what they've really got to offer.'

Twenty minutes later he went out, and walked briskly along the passage towards the lounge-hall. No one was there, except the porter; even the lounge itself was empty. But there were voices outside, a girl laughed, and the party who had been riding came in, two young men and two young women. Engagement rings were glittering on the girls' hands. Both glanced at Grant, as most women did. He appeared oblivious of them, and went out to the drive, looked at the parked cars, then walked round to the back of the bungalow.

Uplands was not only perfectly situated, but admirably run. The building itself was large; he knew that there were thirty bedrooms. There were two wings, east and west, as well as the centre block, where he and Christine had their room. There were paths through the shrubberies, as he remembered, and they stretched for over a hundred yards, towards meadow-land on either side and the orchard beyond.

For a while he walked up a gentle slope, but beyond the swimming-pool the hillside became steeper and the going heavier. He lengthened his stride until he drew near the top of the hill, which was crested by a copse of beech and oak. Then he turned and looked down over Uplands. He could see not only the farmhouse but several cottages on either slope of the valley.

A car came into sight, heading from the main road. The slanting rays of the sun shone on its green sides.

Grant stood quite still, one hand in his pocket, the other clenched in front of him. The car seemed to move very slowly, as if making sure he could recognise it as a green Mercedes. As it drew near the bungalow Grant's teeth clamped together.

It went past.

He relaxed a little, although still watching it. Beyond Uplands a thick belt of trees hid the road, and when the car had disappeared behind them he did not see it again. He waited for some minutes, then took out a slim gold cigarette-case, put a cigarette to his lips and flicked his lighter.

'Excuse me,' a man said; 'will you be so good as to give me a light?'

Grant spun round; the light went out and the cigarette dropped from his lips. The man who had approached him so silently stood a couple of yards away, small, plump, pink-faced, middle-aged. He had pale blue eyes, a snub nose, a rose-bud of a mouth, and no chin to speak of. At first, he had been smiling; the smile disappeared as he added: 'Did I scare you? I *am* sorry.'

'That's all right.' Grant flicked his lighter again, and the other came forward, cupped his hands about the flame, and lit his cigarette. Then he gave a perfunctory smile, and backed away.

'*Thank* you. Isn't it a charming view from here?'

'Very,' said Grant.

'And such a pleasant, quiet spot,' said the pink, plump man. 'I feel that I have escaped the vortex of catastrophic events and come to rest upon the calm beauty of the country. Don't you have that kind of feeling, while you're here?'

'I've only just arrived,' said Grant.

'Well, so have I,' said the other. 'I hope we shall get better acquainted, Mr—'

'Grant.'

'Mr Grant. My name is Prendergast. And I really appreciate this little haven from the turmoil and the strife of the outside world.' He bent his solemn yet childish gaze on Grant. 'I never feel *safe* these days, do you?'

'Oh yes,' said Grant. 'Often.'

'*Do* you?' asked Prendergast. His smile was ingratiating. 'What a fortunate man you are, Mr Grant. I find the condition of the world today creates an atmosphere of constant worry and anxiety, even *danger.*' He uttered the last word softly, there was almost menace in it. 'Of course, it depends so very much on what one does for a living, I suppose. I am an artist.'

Grant looked at him, narrow-eyed.

'And I hope to paint a great deal here,' declared Prendergast. 'Usually I paint portraits.' He gave that word slight emphasis too. 'But I also hope to study and reproduce nature on canvas here. I cannot believe that the peace of this neighbourhood will ever be disturbed by violence, can you?'

Grant said: 'I don't see why it should.'

'True, too true! Shall we walk back?' Prendergast started first; he had a curious little strut. 'So delightful, so serene,' he sighed.

'Don't you exaggerate the violence elsewhere?' asked Grant.

Prendergast looked round at him, blinking.

'Perhaps—perhaps you are right, and it has become an obsession. But—look.' He took a folded newspaper from his pocket, that morning's *Monitor.* He unfolded it, stabbing his forefinger at different headlines. 'Robbery—fraud—hold-ups—violence—racial wars—vendettas—'

He said this while strutting towards Uplands and without once glancing round at Grant, who made no comment and lengthened his stride so as to draw level. They passed the swimming-pool and the tennis courts, and Grant headed for the courtyard. Here, Prendergast paused.

'I go in the other way,' he said. '*Au revoir*, Mr Grant. See you at dinner.'

He beamed, and strutted off.

A small string orchestra played light and lively airs during dinner. The long window of the dining-room overlooked the far side of the valley.

Dusk was falling, and concealed wall-lighting spread a soft glow over the room. There were forty or fifty people here, most of them at tables for two, although one or two larger parties were in the corners. The young foursome which Grant had met was still gay, and wine flowed freely.

Christine had recaptured her radiance of the morning. She wore an off-white gown, with wide puffed sleeves and a square neck. The wine had helped restore her mood of happiness, and to drive fear away. Her grey-blue eyes glowed, while Grant was telling her of his encounter with the little pink artist.

'You look as if all that had gone in one ear and out of the other,' he said, as he finished.

'It didn't, darling, but that little pink man over there keeps looking at me. He must be Prendergast. If you hadn't told me about him, I should have been sure I'd made a conquest. And it's better to keep up appearances, isn't it—if I looked like a frightened fawn, Chin-chin Chinaman would probably celebrate with champagne. Have you found out anything about Pinkie?'

'There hasn't been time.'

Christine put down her glass.

'Mike, I don't mind what happens, I don't terribly mind the mystery, I know you'll explain when you can, but please tell me what you intend to do. Don't try to fight this trouble without telling me.'

'I'll tell you everything from now on. No more posing as a strong, silent man,' Grant promised.

'In small doses I think I should like the pose,' said Christine, with a catch in her breath. 'Darling, would it be unreasonable to say that I'd like to know the worst I can expect. I mean, darling, it would be a kind of revenge if he just spoiled our honeymoon. Do you think that's as far as he'll go?'

Grant said, very slowly: 'I just don't know.'

'It must have been a very nasty business when it started,' said Christine.

'It was,' Grant said, and left it at that. Christine couldn't restrain herself from saying after a pause: 'I don't know that I should like to be left alone for long, Mike; I'm jumpy already. What does one do in the evenings?'

'They'll clear this room for dancing,' Grant told her, and added with a perfectly straight face: 'Or we could have an early night.'

'Why, what a novel idea!' Her eyes laughed at him. 'Let's have a stroll first, the moon might give us ideas.'

There was a half-moon, softening the outline of trees and the hedges, glistened on the swimming-pool, making mystery where there was none and shadows which stretched across the grass on which they trod. They walked close together towards one of the shrubberies.

It was pleasantly warm for an evening in May.

Christine wore a short mink coat, and a filmy scarf over her head. The wind had stiffened, and blew from the west, bringing the strains of the dance-band from Uplands. They weren't the only people out: the foursome had broken up into pairs a few minutes before, and they could hear voices some distance off as they walked along a twisting path through the shrubbery.

'How far does this shrubbery go?' asked Christine, as if it mattered. Only his strength and his nearness did; he was like a drug, making her forget all unpleasant things.

'I'm not sure,' said Grant. 'It seems longer than it is, because the path winds to and fro; I should think it's about—'

His words were cut short, and Christine's fingers bit into his arm, for nearby a girl gave an ear-splitting scream, which sounded hideous on the calm night air.

Chapter Three

Mistaken Identity?

The scream had hardly died away before another shattered the quiet. A man cried: 'What's up?', a girl gasped: 'That's Anne!' There was rustling among the shrubs, then heavy footsteps as of a man running. Another scream started, but broke off, and ended in a gurgling cry. The girl said: 'Tom, don't leave me!'

Grant gripped Christine's arm.

'Let's hurry.'

He half-ran, half-walked with her along the path, twisting and turning a dozen times. Abruptly they came upon another couple, some twenty yards away. Grant called out: 'What's on?'

The couple turned.

'Who's that?' the man demanded in a shaky voice.

'Grant, from the hotel. Have you found her?'

'No,' the young man said, and added in a quieter voice to his companion: 'It's all right, darling. Anne probably saw a fox or something. Anne!' He called her name more loudly. 'Derek! Are you there?'

There was no answer.

'They were ahead of us,' he said, and looked at Grant, apparently relieved when he recognised him. 'Anne's a bit excitable, it might not be anything much.'

'Then why don't they answer?' demanded his companion.

Grant, taller than any of the others, could make out the path clearly as it twisted and turned. A movement farther away caught his eye, and he looked towards it. Some way off a man was hurrying downhill towards the meadows and the road in the valley. He was alone except for something which loped by his side, a huge creature which showed up clearly.

'That—that's not Derek,' muttered the young man.

'Tom, I'm scared,' said the girl, in a shivery voice.

The man named Tom looked at Christine.

'Would you and my fiancée like to go back to the hotel? Then Mr Grant and I could—'

'I'd much rather stay here,' said Christine quickly.

'Oh, I'll stay,' said the girl.

Grant asked: 'Would the others stick to the path?'

'Oh, I think so,' said Tom. 'No point in going off it. We'll lead the way.' He turned and strode along the path, Grant kept by his side, the two girls were close behind. The man and the dog were no longer in sight, but another sound broke the quiet—the stutter of a car engine. Soon headlamps gave a diffused light; the car was travelling away from Uplands and the main road.

None of the party spoke.

A new sound came: a moan. The girl with Christine gasped. Tom glanced at Grant, who pushed on ahead as the moan was repeated. He turned a corner in the path and saw a girl lying near the bushes at one side. She wore a light-coloured dress which was caught up round her knees, and was turning her head from side to side as if in agony. Beyond her, her companion lay quite still.

Grant called: 'Christine, stay where you are a minute.'

Tom went to the girl on the ground, and dropped on one knee beside her, saying: 'It's all right, Anne, it's all right,' while Grant bent over the man.

A glance was enough to show that he was dead; his throat was terribly lacerated, and blood spattered his shirt-front and his coat.

★ ★ ★

Within half an hour of the discovery of the young man's body, a car-load of police had arrived from Shaftesbury, with an inspector, a detective-sergeant and three uniformed policemen. Others had arrived since, as well as a doctor.

The story was now known to everyone.

Anne and her Derek had been walking, close together, when the dog had leapt at them out of the bushes. There had been no warning; just silence, then the leaping figure, which had buried its fangs deep into Derek's throat.

To Christine, everything which had followed held the quality of a nightmare. Grant had said very little, except to the grey-haired manager whom she hadn't seen before, and to the police. The inspector, named Fratton, appeared to have been satisfied with all that had been done since the attack. The hotel residents sat about the big lounge, ill-at-ease.

Christine was in an armchair near the window in the bedroom, with the blinds drawn. Grant stood by the dressing-table, a glass of whisky in his hand.

Christine said flatly: 'He was deliberately murdered, Mike.'

'No doubt about that.'

'He was mistaken for you.'

'It could be,' Grant conceded. He tossed his drink down, and lit a cigarette.

Would *nothing* make him confide in her?

'Have you told the police that?'

'Not yet.'

'You will, won't you?'

Christine spoke tensely, because it was no longer possible even to hope that whoever hated Michael so much would be satisfied with spoiling their honeymoon.

They meant to kill him, and if she was right, an innocent youth had died in mistake for him. And he had talked to her in short, almost brusque sentences, reminding her how little she knew of his past, how little she knew about him.

He pulled up the dressing-stool, placed it in front of her, squatted down, and took her hands.

'Chris, my darling,' he said very quietly, 'I should have told you of this, and postponed our wedding. I couldn't bring myself to, and in a way I'm glad. If anything should happen to me now, you'll be all right for the rest of your life.'

She closed her eyes, because that hurt so much.

His grip on her- fingers tightened.

'But I'm going to have a stab at living,' he went on, with a grim note of raillery. 'That boy's death will be on my conscience for a long, long time.'

'Don't torment yourself with that, Mike! But don't make it worse by keeping it from the police.'

'I'll tell the police,' Grant promised, 'but an hour or two's delay won't make any difference. I—'

Then his voice seemed to fade, for Christine saw the handle of the door turn. The expression on her face made Grant swing round, to see the door opening slowly. He leapt towards it, and Christine held her breath.

Then Prendergast appeared, looking very tired, his face a paler pink. He cried out when he saw Grant, and backed away.

'My dear sir!'

'What the hell do you think you're doing?' Grant towered over him.

'I—I just *had* to come and have a word with you, I really did.'

'Why didn't you knock?'

'I thought you were in the lounge. I was going to wait here,' said Prendergast, unconvincingly. 'I can't bear those other people tonight, they're so devastatingly *earnest*. You are a man of understanding, of intelligence. I could tell that when we met this evening, and I was going to wait for you. Really I was. If—if I startled your wife, I do apologize, but I had to come. After what I was saying earlier about violence, fancy *this* happening.'

'It's remarkable, isn't it?' Grant wasn't mollified, but Prendergast had a skin like a hide.

'Remarkable is hardly the word,' he said. Uninvited, he sat on an upright chair near the wall, and mopped his forehead. Then his gaze fell on the whisky bottle and the syphon on the dressing-table.

Grant turned to the whisky and said: 'Care for a drink?'

'Oh, I would!'

Grant poured out, splashed in soda, and took it across. Prendergast drank deeply.

'Thank you—thank you, indeed, Mr Grant. You're very kind. I feel as if my whole world has collapsed. I thought that here we had found a real haven of peace, that we could forget violence and crime, and yet—such a terrible thing. That poor, young man, struck down in all the splendour of his youth and vigour. Imagine it, Mrs Grant—imagine it if you lost *your* husband in such a way. Imagine the terrors of the nights. Imagine how every time you moved out of the friendly lights of home and the shadows closed about you, you would picture that brute leaping towards you, its ugly great mouth open, its hot breath on your face.'

'You've quite an imagination. Not everyone appreciates it,' Grant said curtly.

'It is always the same with those who have the artistic temperament,' sighed Prendergast. 'One *feels* the pain of others. Take Mrs Grant now. I need only look at her to know that she feels much as I do. Somewhere among her antecedents there must have been an artist, a man of great understanding, great gifts, who passed them on to her—'

Christine jumped to her feet.

'Mike!' she breathed. 'Stop him!' Her face had lost every vestige of colour. 'Please stop him!'

Prendergast stood up, as if startled, blinked from her to Grant, put his glass on the chair and stepped forward.

'My dear young lady, if I have caused you any distress, I am terribly sorry. I am indeed.'

'You draw your pictures too vividly,' Grant said coldly. 'Have the police questioned you yet?'

'*Police?* Questioned *me?*' The pink, plump man looked dumbfounded. 'Why should they?'

'They're bound to question everyone who was outside immediately after dinner.'

'*I* didn't stir!'

'Then I must have seen your ghost,' said Grant.

Prendergast stood staring, his colour deepening from pink to red; and now he looked as if he was afraid.

'I haven't been outside the hotel since before dinner!' he cried. 'I've been here all the time.'

'I saw you outside,' Grant said sharply. 'Perhaps you were carried away by some artistic vision, and—'

'It's a damnable lie!'

'Now don't be absurd. I saw you.'

'It's a lie!' screeched Prendergast. 'I didn't step outside the door!'

He jumped forward, as if to emphasise his protest with a blow. It was absurd, for Grant was so much bigger, but he had made the man lose his head.

Christine realised that he had revealed how much the little artist was living on his nerves, and she sensed the significance of this without really understanding it.

The tension was broken by a tap at the door, and Grant went to see who it was. The tall, comfortable figure of Inspector Fratton stood outside.

Prendergast was so carried away by his rage that he still stood glowering, his feet planted wide apart, his hands clenched and raised.

'*I didn't go outside,* I tell you. Understand that? If you say I did, I'll tell—'

'I'm afraid Mr Prendergast is getting rather excited,' Grant said. 'Come in, Inspector.'

Fratton smiled, as if excitement was one of the emotions which would never affect him. He looked genial, and smiled with a natural affability. Perhaps the expression in his brown eyes as he looked at Grant did something to belie his smile, but his voice was friendly, rich and deliberate with its broad Dorset vowels.

'Excited, is he?' he echoed. 'What about, Mr Prendergast?'

Prendergast didn't answer, but tried to regain his poise.

'He's forgotten that he went outside after dinner,' said Grant dryly. 'I suppose he doesn't want to be in the limelight; artists are such shy, retiring people, but I think you should know everything.'

Fratton actually chuckled.

'That would be a tall order, now, wouldn't it?' he remarked. 'I'd like to know as much as I can, but—'

'It's disgraceful!' snapped Prendergast. 'You are here to investigate a most dreadful crime, and—you laugh. *Laugh!* It is hardly surprising that crime flourishes; the incompetence of the police throughout this land is a crying shame, a scandal, a mockery.'

'Can't live as if I was at a funeral all the time,' Fratton remarked. 'Did you know the dead man, Mr Prendergast?'

'I did not.'

'You'd only met him here,' remarked Fratton.

'Yes.'

'Very humanitarian of you to be so distressed,' said Fratton. 'Did you notice this dog when you were outside?'

'I did not leave the hotel!'

'Oh, of course.' Fratton frowned, and deep grooves appeared on his forehead. 'Possibly you were mistaken, Mr Grant.'

Christine liked the casual way that Michael said: 'I've no reason for saying that Prendergast was in the grounds if I didn't see him, but that's for you to decide. Is there anything I can do for you, Inspector?'

'There are one or two questions I'd like to ask you, sir. No need for you to stay,' Fratton added to Prendergast, 'but I'd like a word with you a little later, if you don't mind.'

Prendergast opened his mouth, as if about to protest, closed it again and went out.

'You seem to have upset him,' Fratton remarked. 'Was it only your saying you saw him in the grounds?'

'Yes.'

'I see. Thank you.' Fratton's expression became positively cherubic. 'You'll both forgive me if I say how sorry I am that this has happened tonight, of all nights.'

Christine dropped into a chair.

'Do all the residents know we're honeymooners?' Grant asked.

'Couldn't say, sir, I'm sure. A lot of information comes my way, of course, and you aren't exactly unknown, Mr Grant.

I'd like to say how glad I am to have this opportunity of meeting you.'

'Thanks,' said Grant dryly. 'Now, how can I help?'

Fratton was bland.

'I thought you'd like to know that we've had a report of a car which passed along this road about nine o'clock, a green Mercedes. There was an Alsatian dog in the back, next to a passenger.'

'Quick work,' said Grant, and Christine watched his strong face and prayed that he would tell Fratton everything now that the opening was made.

'There's a strong feeling among the guests that the dog broke away from his master, and is a mankiller,' Fratton went on. 'Just one of those tragic accidents, like a hit and run on the road. I'm not altogether satisfied that accident is the word, though.'

Grant said: 'I don't think it was an accident, either.'

'Do you think the dog was set on the man?' Fratton was calm and deliberate. 'That would make it murder, Mr Grant.'

'Yes. And I think it was an attempt to murder me.'

'Now that's what I hoped to hear,' said Fratton with engaging frankness. 'I was afraid you weren't going to tell me that, Mr Grant, and I didn't see how I was going to drag it out of you.'

Chapter Four

Flight

'*You knew!*' Christine burst out, and even Grant looked surprised. 'Yes, Mrs Grant, I knew,' said Fratton. 'At least we had a shrewd idea, and that really amounted to the same thing.' Grant laughed a little too loudly.

'I take back all I've thought of the provincial police, Inspector.'

'Oh, we're a much maligned body of men,' Fratton said equably, 'and in some ways I think I can understand it. In a case like this, there isn't much we could do on our own. We're used to our own particular forms of vice and crime, we know the countryside and country people, but if a city-type crime is committed in the country, then we send for Scotland Yard. You didn't realise that some of your recent movements have not passed unnoticed, Mr Grant?'

'I don't follow,' Grant said, but Christine believed that he followed very well. He did not look at her, and he had a sharp, unhappy feeling that he might wish she wasn't present to hear all this.

'Well, sir, you're a public figure, in your own way, you know, and Scotland Yard wasn't unaware of the little difference you once had with Carosi a while ago. Carosi's been in England for several months, and naturally you were watched, just in case he started a vendetta against you. And apparently he has. How long have you been aware of it, Mr Grant?'

'That he was in England—three weeks or so. That he was out for revenge—a few hours.'

'Since the ceremony?'

'On the road this afternoon, but there isn't much I can tell you, Inspector.' Grant told Fratton exactly what had happened with a precision of detail which amazed Christine: he had not missed any trifling thing, and could even describe the painted face in the wardrobe, its colouring, the fact that it was in oils. 'And Prendergast is a painter,' he remarked, and made it clear that he thought Prendergast had been sent by Carosi.

'Ah, yes, sir, I know. Did you in fact see Mr Prendergast in the grounds after dinner, sir?'

Grant grinned.

'No. But an artist had painted that grinning face, and I thought it might be possible to make Prendergast nervous for his interview with you, Inspector.'

'Now if I did a thing like that, I'd be called an *agent provocateur* or something similar,' Fratton said solemnly. 'Planning to spend a few days here, Mr Grant?'

'Like us to?'

'Yes, sir, I would. Only half an hour ago I was talking to Scotland Yard. The truth is that there couldn't be a better spot to lay a trap for Carosi. The hotel can be watched easily, we can check up on everyone who comes and goes without any trouble. You know how badly Carosi's wanted, and you're a certain draw for him. But he's not back in England just for vengeance, sir, he's not that kind of fool. The Yard thinks we can't touch him for what he's done in the past, as there's no evidence. I'm sure you understand, Mrs Grant.'

'Of course,' said Christine.

Grant looked at Christine, very wryly.

'I don't have to, sweet,' he said, 'and it's a hell of a way to start a honeymoon.'

Fratton kept silent.

There was only one thing to do, Christine knew, although as the police knew what had happened she had dared to hope that they could go on. A honeymoon for vengeance. She tried not to show how scared she was, how Fratton had made her realise that Carosi was big enough and evil enough to worry even the police.

'Of course we must stay,' she said, and her smile was a little too bright.

'Thank you very much,' Fratton said, almost humbly.

When he had gone, Grant locked the door, came to Christine, and took her into his arms so very gently; and soon there were only the two of them in the whole world.

Later, when he slept by her side, she realised that he still hadn't told her why Carosi hated him so.

Prendergast was trembling from head to foot when he left the Grants' room, and the sight of a constable on duty outside made him start violently. He hurried to his room, went in and locked the door. He leaned against it, wiping the sweat from his pink forehead. Then he went to a cupboard, took out whisky, and poured himself a stiff peg. He was drinking when the telephone bell rang.

The glass seemed to jump in his hand. The bell kept ringing. He moistened his lips as he crossed the room, took off the receiver and held the mouthpiece against his chest.

'Hal-hallo.'

'What is the matter?' a man asked, in good English with a marked accent.

'I—I am all right,' said Prendergast. 'Nothing's the matter.'

'You sound nervous,' said the other. 'Did all go well?'

'It—well, yes, it—'

'*Did all go well?*' The man's voice sharpened.

'It—no, no, it didn't,' gasped Prendergast. 'I have had a terrible evening, terrible! I have not been able to do much work and—and a terrible thing happened tonight. A young boy was killed—killed! Savaged by a dog. It was terrible! Such a lad—'

The other said softly: 'A *boy* was killed?'

'Yes, yes, that is what I am trying to tell you—'

'We won't talk more now,' interrupted the other. 'I will see you in the morning, as we arranged.'

'I—I will try to come,' said Prendergast. 'The police will ask questions, they may wish to see me, I may not be free to leave.'

'You must be very careful, and not offend the police,' the other said. 'I will see you as soon as I can.'

'That swine Grant,' Prendergast burst out. 'He says he saw me in the grounds tonight. It's a lie, but he told the police, he—'

There was a sharp exclamation; a pause; then: 'I think you had better leave the hotel at once,' the man with the foreign voice said. 'Come, please, at once.' He rang off before Prendergast could say another word.

Prendergast stood very still for a minute or more, only his lips working. Then he moved abruptly, put out the light, and stepped to the window. His room overlooked the hillside and the shrubbery. He drew back the curtains softly. In the distance lights were flashing, and he could just make out the figures of the searching police. They were fools, the police; what could they hope to find now that it was dark? The thought that the police were fools did a little to make him feel better. He put on the bedside lamp, that would look natural enough and began to pack his few clothes. The case wasn't really heavy, but heavy enough, as he had to walk.

He switched out the light again, put the case outside, and climbed out.

Nothing stirred, no one seemed near.

He crept towards the drive, and when he was on the gravel he looked towards the gate. He could just make out the figure of a policeman near the end of the drive. Prendergast went across the drive, and reached the comparative security of the far side, where he was partly hidden from the gate by some shrubs and trees. He trod down tulips and daffodils, without knowing it, and at last reached the meadow.

He walked close to the hedge which bordered the road. At the first five-barred gate he climbed into the road. No one was in sight, and he began to hope that he had escaped from the police, so he had little to worry about now.

After half an hour's walking, he came within sight of the spot where he was to meet the man with the accent. He strained his eyes to try to catch sight of a car parked near the road, and although he could not see one, he was not greatly worried; it would be parked discreetly behind some bushes.

He kept looking behind him, but did not think he was followed.

He reached some cross-roads, and heard a car start up. So it was parked out of sight, and he had been seen; they were ready to take him to safety.

Then a man appeared out of the shadows, right in front of him.

'God!' gasped Prendergast, and went icy cold.

'You need to call upon God,' the other man said, and his right hand moved. The knife was actually sliding into Prendergast's flesh before he realised what caused the searing pain.

He was dead as he fell.

The killer turned and hurried towards the car, parked without lights, and was in it and away before two of Fratton's men, trailing Prendergast, stumbled in the darkness over his body.

'I couldn't bear it if anything happened to him,' Christine thought, and there was fear in her.

Grant, sleeping on his back, was breathing evenly, all unconcerned.

If only she knew more about this man Carosi and his hatred, it might help.

Chapter Five

West Of The Yard

Chief Inspector Roger West of New Scotland Yard knew a great deal about the real reason for the hatred between Michael Grant and Carosi, and was pondering over this, and over the report from Fratton, of the Dorset CID. Sound chap, Fratton. Brilliant chap, Grant! His father was a millionaire, always in the news with spectacular trading deals, and making vast profits. Grant managed to hit the headlines with his own activities almost as often. Big Business didn't always descend from father to son, but here it did. Young Grant's money, looks and record for outstanding courage had made him London's biggest matrimonial prize. He had been proof against all beauty, until he had met the girl whom he had married, after a characteristically whirlwind courtship.

But West was thinking more about Carosi than Grant.

Carosi had lived in London during most of the war. His reputation had never been good, he was known to be on the fringe of many sordid crimes, but for years he had not been suspected as a leader of a vice gang.

It had fallen to West's lot to prepare for the edification of the Home Office, to which Ministry Scotland Yard and all the British police were directly responsible, a comprehensive report on gangs which operated in or from London. He put them into three separate groups.

The first was the race-gang which, despite popular belief to the contrary, did specialize exclusively in race-courses. But it was small-time crime.

In the second group were the 'posh' gangs. There were fewer of these, all members of which were experts at their particular line of business. They comprised the cleverest cracksmen, con-men, forgers, fakers of Old Masters, jewellers and craftsmen, and 'gang' was perhaps the wrong word: there was a ring of them, who had virtually a monopoly of major crimes. There was also a common factor: they did not use violence.

The third group included Carosi's; indeed, it might almost, at one time, have been called Carosi's own.

This was more general than the others, with member-criminals who might easily serve with gangs in either of the other groups, but who were held together by an uneasy allegiance to this particular group. They were almost exclusively led by aliens or by men who had somehow contrived to acquire British nationality, and if they had a speciality, that speciality was vice. All kinds of vice, which riddled London's West End and made it a show place for street walkers.

There was more than vice, of course; much more, and Carosi was a directing genius.

He had been born of an Italian father and an Irish mother.

Nothing was outside the scope of Carosi's activities, and he touched hideous things which the other gangs would not look at. His had been the most powerful gang which had operated for several years, and it had prospered greatly.

For some years Carosi had owned a large country house, to which he retired at irregular intervals with his latest *inamorata,* and a luxury flat in the heart of Mayfair. He had been a familiar figure in the West End, at night-clubs as well as at the most exclusive restaurants. He levied tributes from many dance-bands and night-clubs, from public-houses, even from sections of the big London markets, but he did it with great skill.

The Yard had set many a trap to catch Carosi but had failed.

He had been known to have a set of *dossiers* of rich and of public men, and to extort blackmail. He had always been careful in his choice of victims, but had made one serious mistake. He had blackmailed Sir Mortimer Grant.

The Yard still did not know the skeleton in the financier's armour. They did know that Sir Mortimer Grant had not gone to the police; but he had told his son Michael. Quite cold-bloodedly, Grant had forced his way to Carosi's apartment, and eye-witnesses agreed that afterwards it had looked like a Florida shanty struck by a whirlwind. What was more, Carosi had slipped out of the country, obviously afraid that young Grant could give evidence that would jail him for years.

Grant had never vouchsafed such evidence, and Carosi had not stopped operating by a kind of remote control.

During his absence, the Yard had built up an even more imposing record of the activities he sponsored, and sent several of his associates to jail. But they were still without the proof needed to put Carosi himself inside, and to break up the whole grim, forbidding, menacing organisation.

At nine o'clock on the morning after the murder in Dorset, Roger West entered the office which he shared with four other Chief Inspectors. He was the first to arrive. Five bilious-looking desks and five battered-looking chairs awaited five massive policemen. He looked through his post, then pushed most of it aside, reading over a report which had come from Inspector Fratton by special messenger.

He lifted one of the telephones on Iris desk.

'Is the Assistant Commissioner in?' he asked the operator.

'I don't know, sir, I'll find out.'

'Thanks,' said Roger.

'Yip, he's in,' said a man who had just entered the office. He was tall, with a huge paunch, a long, pointed nose and a receding chin. Whenever he grinned, he showed his prominent teeth. 'Spoke to him myself just now; he walked along the corridor with me.'

'That's a nice start to your day,' said Roger.

'No need to be sarky,' said Chief Inspector Eddie Day, squeezing his bulk between an armchair and a desk, and going to his own place, which was near the window. 'He's all right when's he in a good mood, Chatty is.'

'Let him once hear you call him Chatty, and you'll never know him in a good mood again,' said Roger.

'Gertcha,' said Eddie. 'What do you want him for?'

'Carosi.'

Eddie Day sniffed.

'Put Carosi inside, Handsome, that's what you ought to do—put him inside, no use playing cat-and-mouse with a type like 'im. Go wild and commit bloody murder one day, and once he tastes blood I wouldn't like to say where he'll stop. Here, what's up?' he demanded. 'Have I struck something?'

'There were two murders last night at an hotel where Grant was starting his honeymoon.'

'Cor!' exclaimed Eddie Day, and grinned. 'I'll bet that put an end to *one* sex orgy!'

Roger smiled, stood up, and then picked up the telephone as it began to ring.

'The Assistant Commissioner's in his office, sir.'

'Thanks. Be seeing you, Eddie.'

Roger went out.

He was a fraction under six feet tall, and an exceptionally handsome man, hence his nickname. With his wavy fair hair and fresh complexion, he looked younger than his thirty-eight years, although he was still the youngest CI at Scotland Yard.

He tapped on the Assistant Commissioner's door.

'Come in,' called Sir Archibald Chatworth.

He was alone, a big, burly man with a fringe of grizzled, grey hair, a brown, weather-beaten skin, round face and a permanent scowl, which barely lifted even when he smiled. A farmer behind an office desk.

'Come in, Roger, and sit down.'

Roger obeyed.

'What's on your mind?' Chatworth went on.

'Carosi,' said Roger, and won all the attention he wanted.

'So you want to be off to Dorset?' Chatworth said when the report was finished.

'As quick as I can,' said Roger.

'Yes. No need to worry about formalities; the Dorset Chief Constable called me last night and said he'd be glad if we'd send someone down if Grant intended to stay there more than a day or two.' Chatworth looked at Roger narrowly, then asked in a growling voice: 'Come on, what've you left out?'

'There's a strong streak of coincidence running through the business,' Roger said mildly.

'What is it?' asked Chatworth.

'You know that Michael Grant married Arthur Morely's daughter, don't you, sir?'

Chatworth said: 'Yes. Can't blame the daughter because her father was lucky to get a reprieve after murdering his wife.'

'Morely was at the church yesterday morning—Jameson spotted him,' Roger said. 'He watched the girl, kept his face hidden from her, and went off straight after the ceremony. No fuss, no trouble, but—'

'You mean it's odd that he should have turned up there?' mused Chatworth. 'Natural thing for him to do, surely. I'd say it's a point in his favour that he didn't thrust himself forward so that his daughter couldn't miss him. He's pretty well on his uppers, and might have thought that it would be easy to get some money out of his newly-rich daughter. Hardly a coincidence, though.'

'Arthur Morely was an artist, and maybe he still is. He specialised in portraits. So did Prendergast, who was knifed last night.'

'I see,' said Chatworth. 'H'm, yes. Well, you'd better go down. But don't jump to any conclusions, will you?' he added, almost sarcastically. 'About what, sir?'

'Michael Grant's innocence. These big money barons get high above themselves at times. Sir Mortimer Grant must have a nasty blot on his past to lay himself open to Carosi's blackmail. We never knew that. His son presumably got the incriminating stuff from

Carosi. Did he get anything else?' Roger said: 'I won't overlook any of that, sir.'

'Sure you won't. Keep this in mind, too. We believe Carosi tried to blackmail Sir Mortimer, but the quarrel may have some other basic cause.'

'You mean, when thieves fall out,' Roger said dryly. 'And possibly Michael Grant kept as silent as the sphinx, after discovering whatever the truth was, so as to make sure he didn't give anything away to harm his father. There was talk of one law for the rich and another for the poor when we didn't tackle young Grant for raiding Carosi, remember.' 'Just what's on your mind?' Chatworth asked suspiciously. 'The *Monitor* is the newspaper which began the rumour, and if we bring them on to the inside of this job—'

'You're in charge of the case,' Chatworth interrupted. 'Just remember that regulations say we must treat all the Press without fear or favour.'

'Can we help it if some are more equal to the occasion than others?' Roger asked.

Chatworth said: 'You be careful.'

Roger hurried back to his office, cleared his desk and then telephoned the *Monitor,* asking for a reporter named Fingleton.

He was told that Fingleton was away for a few days, and replaced the receiver thoughtfully.

That morning Roger, with Detective-Sergeant Hubert Gill in his car, and his equipment in the back, made a hurried detour leaving London: he went to his home in Bell Street, Chelsea.

Janet, his wife, was waiting with sandwiches prepared for the journey, and a small suitcase packed.

She looked a little forlorn when he drove off, then poked her fingers through her dark hair, and turned back to the household chores.

Chapter Six

The Bathing-Pool

That afternoon was fine and warm. Michael and Christine left Uplands after lunch to walk across the far hills. They were not surprised that a detective, to whom Fratton had introduced them, followed fifty yards or so behind.

They walked for half an hour, exchanging only a word now and again, until Grant said abruptly: 'We'd better get back. This police shadow almost makes me wish I hadn't said a word to them.'

'It wouldn't have made any difference,' Christine said practically. 'But I suppose we may as well turn back.' She gave a little laugh, not very gay. 'It's funny, this policeman's made us forget that someone we can't see may be watching us, ready for a chance to—'

'Now get this clear,' said Grant, firmly. 'We are not in danger every minute of the passing day.'

'Darling,' Christine said, with a tremor in her voice, 'I don't like being scared. I don't like seeing you edgy, either, and you often are. Don't let's fool ourselves.'

'H'm,' said Grant, and then ignored the police shadow and held and kissed her until she was almost breathless. 'Sweetheart, I don't think there's another woman who would have been as patient as you have,' he said. 'Don't put up with my moods too much, though; half the world and every newspaper will tell you that I've been spoiled. Your job's to unspoil me.' He let her go. 'Now, the story of me and Carosi—'

He told her the story that Roger West had discussed with Chatworth and added very quickly, while they stood looking at each other: 'The blackmail stopped. At Carosi's fiat I found some so-called evidence against my father, and some of information against other people which would have opened a few eyes. I burned the lot, but Carosi didn't know that. He probably thought I'd keep it and use it myself.' Grant looked quite fierce. 'He doesn't know right from wrong, my darling; he's incapable of anything but evil, because to him there's no such thing as right and wrong. There's only money and power. Now! Let me kill another bird while I'm at it. My father's as safe as a pontificating bishop now, and I'm fond of him, even if his heart is made of whatever makes most money at the moment. As mine is! The stuff which Carosi had on him could have ruined him socially. Me, too, because of that Biblical bit about the sins of the fathers. I destroyed the proof but not Carosi's knowledge of it. I didn't intend to stand by and see my father ruined, or see his life made miserable by blackmail. But before young Derek Allen died, it was just a family feud. Now it's very much deeper.'

'Yes, of course,' said Christine, and gave a funny little laugh. 'Will you think I'm heartless if I say our fathers did leave us quite a legacy, didn't they? Mine—'

'That's enough of that!'

'But it isn't, Mike,' Christine said firmly. 'We may not be in the mood for talking about it again for a long time. Whatever your father did, he can hardly have a worse—worse past than mine.' Her eyes were very bright, and she spoke too quickly.

'You know that he lulled my mother and went to prison, you know that he was an artist. Every time Prendergast spoke to me, it seemed as if he were reminding me of that. I've an early photograph of my father, the only one I've seen. He wasn't like Prendergast, but he looked rather plump, and as if he might be pink and fluffy. I was brought up by an aunt and uncle, I've told you all about them. They were kindness itself, but they would never talk about my parents. Darling – it's strange that Prendergast was so like my father, isn't it?'

'That's enough,' insisted Grant. 'If you go on like this I'll think you're suggesting that Prendergast *was* your father, which would be absurd and impossible, as he's still in prison.'

'He isn't,' Christine said.

Grant looked startled.

'No?'

'He was outside the church yesterday morning,' Christine told him. 'But of course he isn't like Prendergast *now*, he's much older. I wouldn't have recognised him, but yesterday morning I had a letter, delivered by hand.' She put her hand in the neck of her blouse, and drew out a crumpled envelope.

Grant stood very still.

'I didn't tell you, I didn't want to spoil the day, and—I was so happy,' said Christine hesitantly, 'and afterwards—well, there wasn't a chance to tell you last night, was there? At the hotel I had a feeling that everything we did was watched, everything we said was overheard. The detective behind us doesn't matter, up here.' She put the envelope into Grant's hands.

He drew out the contents. There was a small sheet of paper, a few typewritten words, and a snapshot which had been taken on a fine day, so that every feature of the subject was there. The man was small, with a deeply lined face, rather pathetic eyes, with a fringe of grey hair.

The note said: '*This was taken of your father a week ago. He was released from prison in February this year.*'

Grant put the photograph back in the envelope.

'You and I ought to get the booby prize for idiocy,' he said. 'Each of us deserves it. We've got to get rid of this crazy idea that we can help each other by keeping personal worries to ourselves. So I'll tell you one more thing, which I was determined to keep to myself to my dying day! Carosi knows your father. He mentioned him when he telephoned two days ago. I preferred not to tell the police that.'

'Mike!'

'It was so characteristic of Carosi that it didn't worry me at all,' said Grant. 'It was just part of his plan to get us on edge, and spoil everything for us—and strike to kill. At least we know everything now.'

Christine's happiness seemed deeper, now, and less dreamlike. There were causes for fear, but no secrets from each other. That was how she had hoped it would be.

It was nearly three o'clock when they entered the hotel.

'Do you know what?' said Grant. 'I'd like a swim. How about you?'

'I'd love to.'

They were laughing and carefree as they passed a tall, fair-haired, good-looking man whom they had not seen before. There was something friendly and attractive about his grin.

In the bedroom, Christine commented: 'He looked interesting, didn't he?'

'For the next week or two, no man may look interesting to you,' declared Grant. 'Rule one for newly-weds.'

'Yes, dear,' said Christine meekly.

Her swimsuit was royal-blue, and fitted snugly, and she caught sight of Michael eyeing her, as if he had never really seen her before.

'There is a time and a place,' she said.

'This is the place,' said Grant, and held and lifted her over the bed, and then dropped her.

'Still want to swim?'

'Later,' she said.

They went out soon after four, wearing their raincoats, and carrying towels. They walked across the flagged courtyard towards the bathing-pool. In spite of the warmth and brightness, no one else was there. Mike took off his coat and began to run when a few yards from the edge. He dived in, as if born to the water, bobbed up and called: 'Come on! It isn't cold.'

Christine poised for the dive.

Even before she started, they heard a sharp report from a long way off. Next moment, something cracked against the side of the bath not a foot from where she stood.

Christine dived, in spite of it. When she broke surface Grant was standing at the shallow end, staring towards the distant woods.

He called: 'Keep low, darling, and swim here.'

She obeyed. They crouched down so that only their heads showed above the side of the pool. By that time, the detective who was guarding them and another policeman had started to run towards the shrubbery.

'So he's still at it,' Grant said, heavily.

He hoisted himself out of the water, and pulled Christine up. They stood watching the policeman, and trying to discern some movement among the trees. They failed, but heard the roar of a motor-cycle engine some way off.

Mike went to the spot where they had left their towels and coats, and brought them back. They wrapped the towels round their shoulders before going to the deep end. One of the surround tiles had a new crack, and a few tiny pieces had been chipped out of it. A little farther away, on the asphalt path which ran round the pool, they saw a shallow groove.

Not far ahead lay the bullet, with its squashed lead nose.

Mike bent down to pick it up.

'Hallo,' a man said, 'found something interesting?'

Both Christine and Mike looked up, and saw the fair-haired man whom they had seen in the hotel.

'I think it's interesting,' said Mike, closing his fingers about it. 'Come on, Chris, we'd better get in.'

'It is a bit chilly,' said the new-comer. 'For more reasons than one. Didn't I hear a shot?'

'Someone fooling about in the woods,' growled Grant. 'Excuse us, please.'

'Of course,' the other said.

'We need a hot tub after that,' Grant said, when he and Christine were in the room. 'You first, darling.' He was very matter-of-fact. 'I hope that blond Adonis won't go blabbing among the others at the hotel. It only wants one or two more attacks like this to cause a panic in the hotel. I'm going to make a genuine sacrifice in the cause of justice,' he added, standing in the bathroom door. 'I'm going to call Fratton, instead of helping you bath!'

Fratton was already at the bedroom door. He took the bullet, said that he hoped his man would find some trace of the man who had fired at them, heard about the young 'Adonis' and smiled rather grimly.

'I don't think you need worry about that,' he said, 'I'll have a word with him. But there's another fellow at the hotel who might really make things difficult—a London reporter, named Fingleton, a big fellow with curly red hair. If he tackles you, I should just say as little as you can.'

'I'll deal with him,' Grant said, as if looking forward to it. Fratton gave his fatherly smile, and went to the door. As he opened it, a man exclaimed aloud.

Standing with his hand outstretched, and looking foolish, was a powerful man with an untidy mop of curly red hair -the hair of the newspaper man, Fingleton. And Fingleton recovered quickly, and actually stepped inside. 'Mr Grant, if you could spare me—'

'Not now, probably later,' said Grant, civilly enough. 'Just tell me this,' begged Fingleton, not in the least put out. 'May I say you're packing everything, including your wife, and flying out of Carosi's vengeful reach?'

Grant looked at him thoughtfully, then moved to the telephone and lifted the receiver.

'Tivern 53, please,' he said, and waited for at least two minutes, while the detective and the reporter looked at him. Then: 'Hello,' said Grant quickly. 'Is that you Haydon? I want you to pack everything again and bring it to Uplands ... Yes, the morning will do. Goodbye.' He rang off. 'That a good enough headline?'

'Hero on Honeymoon,' Fingle said, and his eyes seemed to smile and approve as he hurried off.

'Wise to humour the Press, I always think,' Fratton murmured approvingly. 'I think you're right to stay, Mr Grant, although I'd be the last to blame you if you preferred to leave. No point in ignoring facts. I wouldn't like to be positive that the staff here can be trusted. You fixed up to come here ten days ago, and in those ten days they've had three staff changes. We are checking on the new people, all of whom come from London.'

'Thanks,' said Grant, gruffly.

'Every bit of food you eat is going to be carefully prepared by our chaps,' said Fratton. 'We'll take no chances which can be avoided, and I'm sure you'll be equally careful. Don't drink or take any wine or spirits except out of a bottle you know hasn't been tampered with. All that kind of thing.'

'I hope your chaps can cook,' Grant said dryly.

Fratton said: 'Well, I admire your courage, Mr Grant, I really do. And Mrs Grant's. We'll do all we can but—'

They hadn't been able to stop that shooting at Christine.

Grant didn't go into the bathroom at once. The two visitors had made him even edgier, and he wanted to calm down. Soon he realised that he could hear no splashing, but then, Christine would be out of the bath by now. He looked at her clothes, spread out on the bed.

He called out: 'Going to be long, Chris?'

She didn't answer.

'Chris!' Grant strode across to the door, and turned the handle. She was teasing, of course, proving how ...

The door was locked.

'Chris!' Grant called out, and there was an edge of alarm in his voice. 'Chris, are you all right?'

She still didn't answer.

'*Chris!*' he shouted, and rattled the door-handle wildly. 'Unlock the door; let me in!'

There was no response at all.

He ran towards the passage door and hurried out, calling: 'Fratton—*Fratton!*'

No one answered, although he caught a glimpse of one of the white-jacketed servants, at the end of the passage.

He went to the next room, which also had access to this bathroom, and was part of a suite he intended to take for the rest of the stay here. He tried the handle, but that door was locked also.

He rattled it savagely, and shouted: '*Fratton!* Where the hell are you?'

Fratton appeared, hurrying. Two passing guests looked up, startled to see Grant in his swimsuit, standing and shaking the door like a crazed man. A servant hovered at the end of the passage.

'My wife's locked herself in the bathroom,' Grant said. 'I can't get any answer. There's another way in, through here.'

'Well, don't break the door down,' said Fratton. He slipped his hand into his pocket and drew out a master-key.

They stepped into a room which was furnished like the Grants'. The bathroom door was in the far corner. Mike ran across and turned the handle.

This door was unlocked, and he thrust it open ...

The bathroom was empty.

Christine's towel lay on the floor, in a heap near the swimsuit, which looked a darker blue because it was wet. There were damp footmarks on a cork mat by the side of the bath. The water was still in it, hot to the touch.

The only window was a small, high one, which could be pulled open or shut by means of a long cord: the only exits were through the bedrooms.

Fratton asked in a gruff voice: 'Did she have any clothes with her?'

Grant looked as if he would go mad.

'No. Just the towel—the costume. My God, they—'

'She wouldn't willingly leave the room stark naked,' said Fratton, mildly. 'She must have been forced to go, but she can't have gone far. We'll soon get her back.' He hurried at last, hurrying out of the bathroom and calling over his shoulder: 'Don't touch anything, don't open that other door.'

Grant didn't answer, but stared at the door which led to their bedroom. Bolts at the top and bottom had been shot, but there was no key.

Yet someone had come in here through the other bedroom, managed to overpower Christine and carry her off.

Grant heard a sound behind him. He turned round slowly. Fingleton stood just beside him, pushing a hand through his unruly mop of hair.

'Damnably sorry, Grant,' he said. 'I'll help any way I can.'

Within half an hour of the discovery that Christine Grant was missing, every room in the hotel had been searched, but there was no trace of her. The staff quarters were subjected to the same thorough scrutiny. Members of the staff and all the guests who had been in during the afternoon were questioned. The outbuildings and the garage, the lofts of both the main building and the garage itself were all combed.

There was no trace of Christine.

At five o'clock, dressed in grey flannels and sipping a whisky and soda, Grant sat in his room, bleak-faced, hard-eyed.

The police had found nothing to help in the bathroom; no fingerprints, no footprints which they could photograph. A lot of water had been splashed on the bathroom floor, and there were damp marks on the passage carpet, probably made by a man's footsteps after he'd left, but the marks were not plain enough to be of any use, Fratton told him.

At one end of the passage was the hall: at the other, a blank wall. A porter had been on duty in the hall most of the afternoon. He admitted that he had left the hall several times to answer the telephone, but had never been away for more than two or three minutes. Two of the telephone calls had been for guests; the other had been a wrong number.

'It's just possible that she was carried through one of the bedrooms,' Fratton went on. 'There's one room—at the end of the passage—from which you can get by the window past a blank wall to the other wing. But even that only leads to the servants' quarters. Most of the servants were off duty,'

Grant growled: 'Where's all this leading to? She's missing. We've got to find her.'

'We shall do everything we can,' Fratton said, but the promise sounded empty. 'Everything, Mr Grant, I assure you. There's just one thing I must say. You may hear from Carosi about this. You mustn't lose sight of the fact that he's after you, and Mrs Grant is only incidental to him. Don't leave the hotel without telling us, will you?'

Grant put his cup down.

'I shall do exactly what I like,' he said.

Fratton stood up, looked about to speak again, but changed his mind. He went out, closing the door softly behind him.

Chapter Seven

Missing Bride

The water in the bath had been hot – rather too hot. Hitching herself forward in the bath, Christine had turned on the cold tap, and the splashing had drowned the sound of the door opening, and of the man behind her, who stepped into the room, leaving the door open. She ran her hands through the water to distribute the new patch of cold, then turned the tap off.

The man crept nearer.

He held a large, thick bath-towel in his hands, spread out.

Christine reached forward for her sponge.

The man moved forward again, and with a single sweep brought the towel over her head, pressing tightly against her mouth. She tried to scream, but could not. The pressure eased from her mouth, and tightened on her neck. She couldn't breathe, and the pressure grew worse. Her head began to swim, she felt great pain at her chest, and it was as if she was going to die.

Then everything faded.

The man released his pressure, and, supporting her with one hand, backed away. The lower part of his face was covered with a brown scarf, and he wore a light-coloured raincoat. He removed the towel from her head and shoulders cautiously. Her eyes were half-open and glazed, her lips were parted, and the tip of her tongue showed between her teeth.

He dropped the towel on to the floor, lifted Christine out, and dabbed her body to get most of the water off her skin.

Then he laid her on the floor, on her back, went to the communicating door and shot the bolt quietly, using a handkerchief to prevent fingerprints adhering. Next he took off his raincoat and put it on Christine with quick, rough, impersonal movements. He buttoned the coat high at the neck, made sure that his prisoner was still unconscious, then left her and went across the smaller bedroom, opened the door, and looked into the passage.

The young waiter with dark hair and a long face stood near the entrance hall.

He beckoned. The stranger went back into the bathroom, lifted Christine, and carried her to the room at the end of the passage. French windows led to a small loggia with a blank wall on one side. He went across a small hall and through another doorway which led to the scullery, empty, as it always was at that time of the afternoon.

Outside in the yard, behind the garage, stood a small tradesman's van, with the name *Frost – Fruiterer & Florist* painted on the sides. The doors at the back of the van were open. The man lifted the girl inside, then climbed up behind her and closed the door.

He hadn't seen the driver, who was at the wheel, but the van started off immediately, coasting downhill so as to make little sound.

The man took the scarf from his face, wiped the perspiration off his forehead, and turned his attention to Christine. He laid her face downwards on the floor, and began to apply artificial respiration. It wasn't easy, with the van swaying on the poor road, but after ten minutes, Christine stirred. The man kept on until Christine uttered a little groaning sound. Then he stopped, helped her up, and sat her on an empty crate resting against the side of the van. Her eyes flickered open.

The van reached a small quarry, where a large black limousine was parked just off the road. The man at the wheel of the car waved, the van stopped, and Christine was carried to the car.

'She all right?' asked the car driver.

'She'll do. When I get her in, I'll give her a spot of brandy. Got any car rugs?'

'They're in the back.'

Soon, Christine was sitting up, her head lolling against the upholstery. The man forced a little brandy between her lips.

'It's okay, sister,' she heard her kidnapper say. 'Just go to bye-byes for a bit longer.' He took a hypodermic syringe from his pocket, plunged the needle into her forearm, and pressed his thumb on the plunger.

Fratton was not told of the tradesman's van which had left Uplands until after his talk with Grant. Then a kitchen maid mentioned it to a policeman. She hadn't thought it worth worrying about, because the van came so often, and the driver was usually the same.

Had she seen him?

No, but that didn't mean anything; he always took the flowers into the scullery and left them in a pail.

Fratton put a call out to all police patrols and AA and RAC scouts.

By six o'clock, the florist was discovered, bound hand and foot in a quarry, and the van was found parked just off the road.

No one had seen the black car there.

Fratton left the telephone in the small room that had been set aside for the use of the police, and went into the entrance hall.

Roger West was talking to the porter, but broke off when Fratton arrived.

'Finished?' he asked in a sharp voice.

'As far as I can be,' growled Fratton.

'Yes, it's a pretty poor show,' said Roger, bleakly. 'I know the one about not crying over spilt milk, but this is enough to float a battleship.'

'Don't rub it in,' Fratton growled. 'They did a damned good job, too. Couple of strangers were near the gate, distracting my man there. He made the van stop, and actually looked in through the back windows. If there was anyone beside the driver, he must have crouched under the driver's seat. But clever or not, it's hell for us.'

Roger said more mildly: 'No one will have your blood, anyhow. The *Monitor* will flay me and torture Grant, but it won't hold you up to ridicule. There's another thing to remember. Carosi's gang has specialized in girls. Most of them were empty-headed, little fools with pretty faces and busty figures, who asked for trouble but got a lot more than they bargained for, or deserved. If I were told that Carosi had sent a hundred out of the country, and that they're now living in Algiers, Buenos Aires or Montevideo, wishing they'd never been born, I wouldn't disbelieve it.'

Fratton drew in his breath.

'That bad?'

'That bad.'

'Michael Grant know that?'

'He knows it.'

'Now I can understand the look in his eyes,' Fratton said.

'So can I.' Roger glanced towards the passage and caught a glimpse of Grant, who withdrew his head quickly, and stood just out of sight. 'We can take it that Carosi snatched Mrs Grant instead of having her killed, just to add to Grant's torment. But there's a credit item: she is alive.'

'How can you be sure?'

Roger said, slowly, heavily: 'I'm backing the obvious. They wouldn't have carried a corpse away, and it would have been easier to have killed her in the bath. I'm not sure that in the long run this won't help us,' he added, moodily.

'Oh, nonsense!'

'This thing's going into the Press in a big way,' Roger reminded Fratton. 'It will shock the public conscience. There'll be more outcries against the vice laws as they stand, but it will also focus attention on Carosi, and will worry a lot of his small fry.'

'I suppose it's possible—' Fratton began.

'It's a hideous suggestion,' Grant rasped. He stepped out of a doorway; obviously he had been hiding. 'Who the hell *are* you?' His glare at the kidnapper could not have been fiercer; and his eyes burned as if with tormenting fire.

'This is Chief Inspector West of New Scotland Yard,' Fratton said hastily. 'He—'

'So the *Yard* allowed this to happen,' Grant said harshly. 'I'll see you're slated all right, West. I'll use every bit of influence I have to push you back in the ranks.'

'At the time Mr West was out in the grounds a long way—' Fratton began.

'His job was to protect my wife,' Grant said in a quivering voice. 'I don't care who suffers, provided I get my wife back. If I have to break you both to do so, I'll break you.'

The man was living in hell, Roger knew, and undoubtedly felt worse because he was blaming himself. It must be purgatory to know that he had been within yards of his wife when she had been kidnapped. But it was time to put the bridle on him, to pull him up. There was Fratton looking ten years older, and Fingleton about to set Fleet Street by the ears, and Carosi, laughing his head off.

'So if you know what's good for you—' Grant went on.

'Ever thought of blaming yourself?' Roger asked, so softly that the words seemed to catch up on Grant very slowly. 'Ever asked yourself how many people have suffered from Carosi because you let him go free?'

Fratton stood open-mouthed.

Grant was shaken out of his fury.

'You must be crazy! Why—'

'I'm not crazy about this, Mr Grant. You raided Carosi's flat, you found records of his crimes, but you didn't do a thing about it for fear your father would pay for his past sins,' Roger said. 'Now all you can think about is your wife. Well, I can think further. I can think of all of Carosi's victims, past, present and future. I can think of making him pay for what he's done already, and stopping him from ruining more men, breaking more homes, luring more girls abroad on phoney night-club deals. Like it straight? I'll do everything I can, every policeman in the country will do all he can to get your wife back. We'll do it because it's our job. We'll do it because we want to help both you and her, as well as all the other poor devils.'

Grant stood silent; stunned.

'Nothing will stop you trying to find your wife on your own,' Roger went on, 'but don't listen to ransom talk, or Carosi's promises. If you do, you may be cutting your wife's throat.'

'What makes you think he'll get in touch with me?' Grant made himself ask.

'Because she's a bargaining weapon while she's alive,' Roger said; and then his voice and manner seemed touched with compassion. 'I think we'll find her.'

But the dread in Grant's eyes told him that Grant had little hope.

Chapter Eight

Waking

It was dark.

Christine lay on something soft, a couch or a bed. Her eyes were painful and her head ached. She groped about the couch, and felt the edge, and the sheets and blankets. There was a quilt too, and she touched a hot-water bottle with her foot. So her captors were looking after her.

If only there were a glimmer of light ...

One came.

It appeared in front of her eyes, just ahead of her – a faint outline of a door against pale light. It made her calmer. She dozed off, and kept waking at intervals. She realised that she was suffering from the effects of the drug, that before long she would wake up and not want to go to sleep again. But now, she felt no fear.

She woke from an uneasy sleep, and was aware of a different light. She looked towards it. There was a heavy curtain over the window, but some daylight forced its way through. It wasn't enough to show her the room clearly, and she stretched out her right hand towards a bedside lamp. She pressed the switch and the glare of the light made her close her eyes, but soon she opened them again.

It was a small room, luxuriously furnished, but very different from the room at Uplands. The ceiling was much higher. The divan bed on which she lay was exquisitely comfortable. The carpet, of pale blue and cream, was thick and rich. A dressing-table of wrought-iron, painted cream, had on it a small mirror with an iron frame, the most modern style.

She had on a sleeveless nightdress of pale-green silk, with lace at the neck and the shoulders. It wasn't hers. Slowly, she recalled the attack, and shivered at the recollection; then her mind began to work very quickly. Someone had put the nightdress on, put her to bed, taken great care of her.

Why?

Who had kidnapped her?

And why?

She remembered – Carosi.

And Michael.

He would be in torment, blaming himself, trying to tear down the world to find her. How little and yet how well she knew him!

There was that youth, with the savaged throat.

And the attempt to shoot her, at the pool.

She sat up, put out a leg, put a foot to the floor, then stood up. She swayed, helplessly. The effort of moving had made her head ache far worse, and slowly she lay down again. She wished that she hadn't moved, for her head thumped with pain. Her mouth was parched, and when she ran her tongue round it, seemed furry.

The door opened.

A girl came in, and closed it.

A girl?

A woman.

The woman looked at Christine with a frown, then saw that she was awake, and smiled.

It was a curious smile, in a face which was very white, and in eyes dark with mascara. Her lips were brightly painted, too. She walked rather mincingly across the room, and said: 'Hallo, dearie, feeling a bit better?'

She had a coarse but quite friendly voice; no viciousness, no evil.

'Yes, I'm all right,' Christine muttered. 'I'm thirsty, that's all.'

'That's okay then, we can let a bit of daylight in,' said the newcomer. She minced across the room and drew the curtains. The daylight reduced the bedside lamp to a dim yellow, and the woman came and switched it off.

'Now, now,' she said, reprovingly, 'you've been trying to get up, and you shouldn't, you know. Crikey, look! Your eyes are all bloodshot, you must have a splitting head. Like a cup o' tea?'

'Oh, I would!'

'Okay, then, I'll get one,' promised the other. 'Won't be long. Don't do anything silly, dearie, it can't help you.'

She went out; and Christine heard the key turn in the lock.

It was a kind of prison, in spite of that unexpected 'nurse'. How long would she be gone?

Footsteps soon came near again. A key grated in the lock, the door opened, and the woman returned, carrying a tray. She put it down on a chair near the door, slipped the key into a pocket in her dress, then brought the tray over to the bed and put it on the bedside table.

'Let it draw a minute, dearie,' she said, sitting down. 'It'll do you more good then. You're looking a bit better, I think; you'll soon be okay. Morphine makes you feel like that, but you were lucky—he looked after you. You're in one of the best bedrooms. I wish I had half your luck, you must have caught his eyes proper. Takes some pleasing, he does—I wouldn't do for him. Not me. He never liked bow legs, either!' She gave a little giggle. 'What's your name?'

'Christine Morely.' As soon as she had said 'Morely', she realised that it was Grant.

'Chrissie'll do for me,' said the other. 'I'm Maisie, ducks. Been here quite a long time, and it's all right when you get used to it. I should think the tea's about right now,' she continued, and poured out the tea.

Christine let a mouthful cool slowly inside her mouth, and then let it move from cheek to cheek before swallowing it. She took increasingly large sips, until the cup was empty, while Maisie talked and drank, and 'he' and 'him' were always on her lips.

'Who is this he you keep on talking about?' Christine made herself ask.

Maisie stared. 'Who *is* he? Don't be daft, Chrissie.'

'But I really want to know.'

'Cor strike a light!' said Maisie, and drew back a little. 'Sorry, dearie, but if you ain't been told, I'll leave the telling to him. I've been smacked down too often for speaking out o' me turn.'

'Is he here?'

'Not just yet, but he will be soon.'

'Are we in London?'

'You can ask him all the questions you like, but it's no use asking me,' said Maisie, quite firmly. 'I'm here to do what I'm told, see. How about a wash and a bit of make-up on? Your nose is so shiny, I can see my old pan in it. Here, let me give you a hand.'

It was strange to sit in front of the mirror and to watch the reflection of Maisie actually brushing her hair – as if she liked the feel and the sight of the wavy tresses. At last she finished, took the tray, went out and locked the door.

Christine sat on the divan, her legs curled up beneath her. She felt better, her mouth was no longer parched, and her head hardly ached at all, but she was dizzy with bewilderment.

She hated to think, but she had to. Of Mike ...

The door opened again, and she had plenty of warning, because the key turned in the lock. She expected to see Maisie, but it was the young waiter from Uplands. He was dressed in his white jacket, and with his oily mop of hair and his long, unsmiling face, he looked exactly the same as he had at the hotel.

He carried some newspapers, put them on the bed, then turned and went out.

Christine stared at the locked door for a long time before she touched the newspapers, then suddenly snatched them up.

Chapter Nine

Carosi?

Christine's own face stared up at her from the front page of the *Monitor.* Her wedding photograph. It was like reading about someone else.

Fingleton had described vividly what the police imagined had happened, and had managed to get a photograph of the bathroom, showing her swimsuit and the crumpled towel on the floor. Another picture caught her eye, of the remarkably handsome man she had seen at Uplands. The caption read:

> *'Chief Inspector Roger West of the Yard, who has been summoned to Uplands by the local police. Accompanying him is Detective-Sergeant Gill.'*

Christine looked through the inside pages of the newspaper, and was aghast to find an article about Carosi and Mike. There, in garbled form, was the story of the encounter between Grant and Carosi. There were lurid details of Carosi's reputation, of the fact that he was suspected of so many different crimes.

After she had first looked through all the papers, she noticed that some paragraphs were faintly marked with pencil. One mentioned that Carosi was suspected of white slavery; another emphasized the fact that he trafficked in drugs; a third, that he was suspected of being one of an international vice ring.

Each of these hints heightened her fears.

She put the papers down at last and closed her eyes. Her nerves were quivery. If Carosi came into the room now, she would scream – she wouldn't be able to help herself. She knew so much more about him now.

There was a faint sound, and she opened her eyes.

Carosi stood at the end of the divan.

Christine hadn't heard him come in, hadn't heard a sound; but there he was. The man of the car; the man whose picture had hung in the wardrobe. Chin-chin Chinaman. He stood there like a statue, without speaking, without grinning.

She seemed frozen. She could not move, could only stare at him.

Why didn't he move? Speak? Do something, *anything* – instead of just standing there, within a foot of the divan. He seemed to be staring through her – no, to be stripping her with his eyes. She felt as if she were in the presence of something unclean.

The door behind him closed.

Just when she thought that she could not stand it any longer, when she felt a scream forming in her throat, his lips moved.

He spoke in a peculiar voice, as if he had a severe cold.

'So, Mrs Grant,' he said.

Three simple words; and yet he managed to put evil into them, to touch each one with horror. There was a sneer and a malice in them. 'So, Mrs Grant.' Just that, and it seemed to emphasize her helplessness, to remind her that she was completely in his power, that there was nothing he could not and would not do.

'You are comfortable?'

Three more sneering words. 'You are comfortable, but you will not be for long,' he might have said. 'You must not be stubborn,' he said aloud, and moved nearer.

Her scream came out, high, shrill.

Carosi did not change his expression as he looked intently into her eyes, and he did not stop moving. He drew near to the side of the divan and then put out his arm and pressed her gently at the breast. Gently. Gently, but with such a threat of what he could do.

'You are comfortable?' he said again.

'Yes—yes!' she gasped. 'Thank you, I—thank you.'

'You will remain comfortable if you are not difficult,' he said, as if speaking hurt his throat. 'I do not want you here alone for long; I wish your husband to join you. You will do exactly what you are told. You understand?'

'Yes!'

'I hope that you do,' said Carosi, very precisely, 'because if you do not, you will not be comfortable.'

Now, he eased the terror a little, perhaps because he made it seem that he meant just what he said. She could not think of Michael, only of her terror.

'You have read the newspapers?' he asked.

'Yes—yes, of course!'

'I bring you something else to read,' said Carosi.

He took a slim volume from beneath his coat. The title meant nothing to her: *Records*. She stretched out for the book because he seemed to expect it, and he appeared to be going to let her take it, then snatched it away and tapped her across the head with it. A corner caught her in the eye, which began to sting and to water, and involuntarily she closed the other eye. She couldn't see him, couldn't see what he was going to do. She pressed one hand against the stinging eye and made herself open the other. She could only see through a mist of tears, couldn't see clearly, still couldn't see him.

And then she could see.

He had gone, without a sound.

She lay in a daze for a long time, and then began to realise the significance of what he had said, of the awful danger for Mike. She didn't want to think about it. She clenched her hands, and her fingers touched the book which he had left beside her.

Records.

She opened it at random, to do anything but think.

There were two photographs, each taking up a full page. On the left-hand side was a young girl dressed in a swimsuit. She looked no more than twenty, and promised all the gaiety that one would expect in a young girl. On the opposite page was another photograph of a woman, dressed in a cloak which reached the ground. Her face looked old and careworn. She was smiling, and that made the expression worse, there was only misery in her; it was as if someone had ordered her to smile and she had tried, but the camera had seen through the twist of the lips to the unhappiness beyond.

Beneath this photograph was a date: 1949. And beneath the other another date: 1943.

Then suddenly she realised the truth; this was the same girl – photograph taken six years after the other.

Unsteadily, Christine turned to other pages. On every left-hand side were pictures of young girls; on the other side hags.

She turned to the front of the book, and saw only the two words: *Buenos Aires*.

When she had been in the room alone for another hour, the quiet outside was disturbed by an unfamiliar sound, one she had not heard since she had been here. It was the barking of a dog. Yet it was hardly a bark, but a deep-throated roar such as might come from the throat of an Alsatian, like the one which had killed Derek Allen.

There was no real comfort here; only horror.

The day which followed the kidnapping of Christine Grant was a bad one for Scotland Yard. The newspaper accounts were exasperating, but the real trouble was that everyone felt that the Yard had let itself down. A cartoon in a newspaper showing Christine Grant barely covered in a towel being led past several policemen who were peering into some bushes, was the worst gibe.

No one pilloried Roger West: it was as if police and pressmen knew he was bitterly angry with himself. But the real cause of the depression was the fact that no one had any idea where Carosi was, and everyone known to have worked for him had gone to ground.

London was searched as it had seldom been, and none of Carosi's men was found.

Flats and apartments had been left completely empty. Men and women who normally could have been picked up in restaurants, clubs and pubs had vanished.

The disappearances created a strange, unfamiliar uneasiness throughout the Yard.

Roger West had spent the day with Fratton, Lane and others, covering the Dorset end. A pathologist from the Home Office arrived to examine Derek Allen's body, and a prominent veterinary surgeon had also been consulted. The fact that the dog was an Alsatian was established.

The atmosphere of tension and uncertainty at Uplands remained, heightened now that everyone knew who Roger was, because of newspaper photographs. But Detective-Sergeant Gill, although on the premises, was not known as a policeman, except by Fingleton, who did not talk.

Gill was now a 'waiter'.

Roger went to the room which had been set aside for the police, and pressed the bell.

Gill, looking large and awkward in his white jacket and black trousers, was a fresh-faced, fair-haired man with broad features, and a nice sense of humour.

'You rang, sir?' he asked, with a straight face.

'That's right, waiter,' said Roger. 'Sit down a minute, and tell me if you've got anything.'

'There's one curious thing,' said Gill, obeying. 'One of the waiters, a youngster named Luigi, was off in the early afternoon yesterday, came back on duty at tea-time, and worked late. He was due for duty again this afternoon, but hasn't turned up. He's only been here about a week.'

'What have you done about it?'

'As you were out, I telephoned the Yard.'

'Good. What's this Luigi like?'

'Looks about eighteen, is tall, slim, with a long face and dark hair,' said Gill. 'Never had much to say for himself; I haven't had as much as a word with him. Derek Allen's friend, Grayson, has been poking in and out of the kitchen asking a lot of silly questions.'

'I shouldn't stop him,' said Roger, 'it'll ease his mind, if nothing else. Right, go back and wait!'

Gill went off, grinning, and Roger immediately put in a call to the Yard. He was put straight through to Chatworth, who asked abruptly: 'Anything new?'

'Not to call new, sir,' Roger said. 'We're after a missing waiter—'

'Named Luigi. I know that.'

'I'd like a long talk with him,' Roger said grimly, 'and I'd also like a word with Mrs Grant's father.'

'Why?'

'Grant tells me that Carosi tried to upset him on the telephone by talking of Morely and his past, and on her wedding morning Mrs Grant was sent a snapshot of her father. A characteristic Carosi trick. We've no evidence that Carosi is actually using Morely, but he might be.'

'If he is, then Morely's probably disappeared with all the others,' growled Chatworth.

'We could find out, sir.'

'I'll arrange it,' promised Chatworth. 'Is there anything else?'

'I don't think so, thanks.'

'Well, I've something for *you*,' said Chatworth. 'Sir Mortimer Grant is using all his influence to make things really unpleasant, so don't be surprised if you get a very bad press tomorrow.'

He rang off.

Roger replaced the receiver, lit a cigarette, faced the task of re-reading all the reports, and felt gloomy and on edge. It wasn't pleasant to have to sit back and wait for Carosi to act, and it almost amounted to that.

There was another angle which he liked even less. It wasn't nice to think of Christine Grant in Carosi's hands. He could turn her into a dopey in a few days, or make this 'honeymoon' a thing of horror and revulsion. The fact that Fratton had been nominally in charge didn't absolve him, Roger. If they didn't get her back soon, he was going to have a long-lived burden on his conscience.

Carosi had taken her as bait for Grant, of course, and Grant was being closely watched. If he made a move ...

Just before seven o'clock, there was a tap at the door, and the Yard man named Lane came hurrying in, and said: 'I thought you ought to know this at once, sir. Grant had a telephone call five minutes ago, and he's getting his car out of the garage.'

Chapter Ten

Grant Takes A Chance

The man who spoke to Grant on the telephone had a stilted voice, and sounded as if he were not used to speaking English. He did not say much, but every word hammered itself into Grant's mind. Mrs Grant was 'safe'.

She would not be hurt if Grant did exactly what he was told. The first order was vital: he must not tell the police about this call.

He must leave Uplands immediately.

He must drive to Salisbury.

If he were followed, he must go to the Castle Hotel, have a drink, and then return to Uplands. If he were not followed, or could shake off any pursuer, he was to go to Salisbury Railway Station and enter the buffet on the down platform from London.

He would meet someone there whom he would recognise, and from whom he would get further instructions.

Grant had been standing by the side of the bed when the call had come through, and he stayed there for a few tense seconds, staring out into the gathering dusk.

He turned away suddenly, went out, passed two or three of the guests without looking at them, and went outside. It was cool: almost chilly. He did not look round, but went to his car and backed it out of the garage. A policeman on duty at the gates glanced at him, but did not attempt to stop or speak to him.

Grant turned left, towards the main Salisbury–Shaftesbury road, and trod hard on the pedal.

For the first time he looked behind him, and saw the sidelights of a car moving down the drive. So the police were following. The road ahead was straight although narrow, and his speedometer needle quivered until it reached the eighty mark. The half-light made it a strain to drive, but he didn't put on his lights. He could still see those of the car which he imagined West was in, but it seemed farther away. He reached the main road, and three miles from Salisbury he turned off. Now he had to have his lights on.

He knew the district well, and made no false turnings. Forty minutes after he had left Uplands, he approached Salisbury along the Amesbury road, feeling quite sure that the police would not expect him to enter the town from the north.

He reached the railway station, and pulled up halfway along the station approach. This was a parking place, and he switched off the lights and got out. He walked towards the booking-office, and stood looking towards his car. A policeman was standing not far away, but took no notice of him.

After five minutes, Grant went into the booking-hall.

It was dimly lit. No trains were due, for the platform wasn't crowded. He got a platform ticket from a slot machine, then went on to the arrival platform from London.

The light in the buffet was better than on the platform, but he saw no one whom he recognised. He ordered a bitter, and stood by the bar, drinking.

The door opened, and a mild-looking, little man appeared. Grant hardly spared him a second glance.

The little man went to a table near the window, and sat down. When he looked up, Grant saw him full-face. Mild grey eyes were turned towards him without any sign of recognition, but there could be no doubt that this was the man Grant had come to meet.

It was Arthur Morely; Christine's father.

Grant went to the table and sat down. Morely greeted him with a faint smile, and continued to sip his tea. The muscles on Grant's cheeks tautened, and he was clenching his fists. Morely took out a paper packet of cheap cigarettes: there were only two inside. He put one to his lips and then patted his pockets, stopped, looked disappointed, and said: 'Excuse me, sir—*have* you a match?'

'Match?' Grant hesitated, then took out his lighter and thumbed it. Morely lit his cigarette.

'Thank you. It's a cool evening, isn't it?'

'You're cool,' Grant growled. 'What do you want?'

'Please,' protested Morely, '*please*. We must be careful. I have a message for you, of course, but we must be careful.' He sat back in his chair and smiled at the tea-girl, while Grant toyed with his glass.

Morely said with soft precision: 'I do not want to cause delay, but I must be careful. I have been told exactly what to do, and I must obey, Mr Grant. So must you. My daughter's life may depend on it.'

Grant said nothing.

'And I am waiting to hear from a friend,' said Morely. 'He or she will tell me whether the police have followed you here. If they have, then you will have to return to Uplands and wait for another message.'

Words seemed to be forced out of Grant.

'Do you know where she is?'

'No, Mr Grant, they have not confided in me; they are doubtless afraid that if I knew, I would inform the police at once. As indeed I should. I am terrified of these people. The very thought of crime distresses me, and this one is so much worse because it affects my own daughter.'

'You may have to be here, but you don't have to be a nauseating hypocrite,' Grant growled.

'Hypocrite?' echoed Morely, softly. 'Don't judge me too harshly, Mr Grant. I spent so many years in prison, terrible years of bitter self-reproach, while expiating a terrible crime. Today I might have been judged insane. A psychiatrist might even have prevented it. There was one gleam of light in the dark misery of my prison life. My daughter, now your wife. I dreamed of her being happily married, the only dream I had. When I came out of prison and found that there was every prospect of this becoming true, I knew the promise of happiness again.'

There was no easing in Grant's expression.

'You may find it hard to believe, but it is the solemn truth,' Morely assured him. 'I was determined to see her on her wedding day. I was outside the church, but did nothing to attract her attention, to mar her radiance. When I saw her, I felt that I could go away in peace.'

A train approached, rumbling loudly; someone shouted; the train whistle shrieked as it hurtled through the station. Morely did not speak again until the roar had faded.

'And then I heard from Carosi,' he said.

Grant caught his breath.

'I had heard of him before,' went on Morely, still softly. 'You would be astonished if you knew how many things are talked about in prison. Some of this evil man's associates were in the same jail as I.'

Morely stubbed out his cigarette. Two or three more people came into the buffet, there was a clatter of glasses and cups.

'Perhaps you can imagine how shocked I was to hear from such a man,' Morely went on, and there seemed the shadow of horror on his face. 'I am not a criminal, but of course I am branded for life. Carosi knows this well. I was told to come here and talk to you, and warned that if I did anything to upset the plans, Christine would suffer. As I had read the newspapers, I knew what had happened to Christine. Could I do anything but obey?'

His voice was gently pleading.

Grant said: 'If it's—' He broke off, and a word came explosively, 'money—'

'No. Thank you,' said Morely, simply. 'I do this for fear; not gain.'

A middle-aged woman came bustling in, carrying a furled umbrella, wearing an old-fashioned straw hat and a dark-blue coat. In her right hand was a wicker-basket. She went to the counter, ordered tea, and brought it back to the table.

Morely looked at her as though he were mildly interested.

Grant asked gruffly: 'How long shall we have to wait?'

'No longer; that is the messenger,' declared Morely. 'It *is* all clear now; I may give you the message. You are to take the next London train, which leaves at 8.15. At Waterloo you must go to the escalator which leads to the Underground railway, and wait on the near side of the bookstall downstairs. Is that quite clear?'

Grant didn't speak.

The red-faced woman sipped her tea noisily.

'*Do* you understand?' demanded Morely urgently. 'The train won't be long, and you have to get your ticket. And you are not to communicate with the police, and I beg you not to, because you are being watched. All the time you are being watched.'

'I understand,' Grant said, and added abruptly: 'If you ever get a chance, will you take a risk to help your daughter?'

'I would lay down my life for her,' Morely said.

Telephone message from Chief Inspector West, from Salisbury to Scotland Yard:

> *Don't pick up Morely he is being followed stop. Using facial disguise am personally following Grant from Salisbury in Waterloo direction stop. Advise Grant being trailed taking extreme precautions not to be observed stop.*

A surge of people passed Grant as he waited near a bookstall at Waterloo, which was closed, and pretended to read an evening paper. A boy pushed past him.

Grant looked down on a bare, cropped head, and saw the lad's knowing grin. Then he was startled to see a slip of paper held in grimy fingers.

'Cost yer 'arf a quid, guv'nor.'

'What is it?'

'Expecting a message, aincha?'

Not until a ten shilling note was in the boy's hand was Grant allowed to take the paper. The boy slipped off among the crowd. Grant raised his newspaper, and unfolded the note inside it. One sentence was scrawled in pencil: *Go to Victoria Station, under the clock.*

There were two clocks at Victoria.

Grant stood statue-like beneath one for five minutes, before he remembered the other. He walked swiftly across to the second, but when he reached it, hesitated and began to walk back. *The* clock – the fools, why hadn't they specified which?

A woman approached him, flouncing along, raddled face heavily painted. She muttered something under her breath, and Grant said harshly: 'No, go away.' She grinned into his face, and rested her hand on his arm. He pushed her away, but she held his hand. He felt something hard in it. When she had minced on, he looked down at a railway ticket which she had pressed into his hand.

It was a first-class single to East Croydon.

Grant wiped the back of his neck as he moved away from the clock. He went towards the nearest ticket barrier, and asked a porter where the Croydon trains started.

Telephone message to Scotland Yard from Chief Inspector West:

Grant at Victoria Station, accosted by small boy and a street walker. Heard to ask for Croydon. Request urgent instructions all Surrey, Sussex, Kent police to watch all roads and to use radio patrol-cars where possible. Request radio car await me at each of the three Croydon railway stations.

Grant reached East Croydon just after eleven-forty-five.

Under the lights the platform looked deserted as the train drew in, but a crowd of passengers alighted, and he found himself caught up among them. Having no orders to wait, he passed through the barrier. Two or three taxis were standing in the Yard, and a driver said: 'Taxi, sir?'

'No,' said Grant. There was a light over the exit, but otherwise the station approach was gloomy. Most of the passengers had gone now, only a few who had come from the end of the train hurried by.

All the taxis were driven off.

At the far end of the station approach stood a car. Its rear light seemed very bright. No one came from it. Another, bigger car, turned into the approach, and the headlights shone on Grant. The car headed straight for him, and he put up his hand to shield his eyes. The lights slewed round as the car made a half-circle and pulled up opposite him.

A chauffeur beckoned him.

Grant went forward, with long strides. The chauffeur put his hand back to open the door, taxi-driver fashion. Grant got inside and nearly fell over a foot.

'It's all right,' a girl said. 'Sit down.'

He could just see her, in the corner.

The car started off, and he just saved himself from falling into the girl's lap. She had a youthful face, classical, oddly immobile. He caught another glimpse of her as they passed beneath street lamps in the main road, but the car soon turned off into an unlit road.

Radio message from Chief Inspector West to all police patrol-cars for general use Surrey, Sussex, Kent:

Grant in chauffeur-driven Armstrong–Siddeley, black or dark blue heading south from Croydon. Report progress stage by stage but do not follow closely.

Chapter Eleven

Destination

'Where are we going?' Grant asked, but he did not expect an answer.

'You'll see,' said the girl.

Grant felt for cigarettes. 'Will you smoke?'

'No, thank you.'

Grant put a cigarette to his lips and flicked on his lighter. The cigarette didn't matter: seeing the girl more clearly did.

She was young, and very good looking. The hair beneath a small hat was dark.

Grant lit the cigarette and put out the light.

'Satisfied?' the girl asked.

'I like to know my company,' Grant said.

They were now out of the built-up area, travelling along a wide, main road. In the glow from the headlights of approaching cars, Grant saw factories on either side. There was something familiar about this stretch. They passed over a bridge and he leaned forward, looking towards the right, and heard a new sound, the roar of a plane flying very low.

This was Croydon Airport, or very near it.

Was he to fly abroad?

Yes, there was the airport ...

The car went past, without slackening speed.

'No, we're not going to the airport,' said the girl, without looking at him.

'Where *are* we going? To my wife?'

'It really matters like that?' There was a note of incredulity in the girl's voice.

Grant stared at her profile, illuminated for a moment in the light of a passing car. Now he was sure about her. She was lovely, cold, hard-faced. He looked at the chauffeur, driving so casually, only a foot or two away from him, in front of the glass partition. If he were to put his hand round the man's neck, he would be able to tell the fellow exactly what to do.

'I have a gun in my hand,' the girl announced calmly.

Grant could just make out the pale shape of her arms and her hands, resting in her lap. He couldn't see the gun, but felt sure that she had one.

'If you ever get a chance of seeing your wife again, it will depend on the way you behave,' she said quite flatly. 'If there should be any trouble here, or if you should be followed—'

'How well do you know Carosi?' Grant asked abruptly.

'Well enough to know that if anything goes wrong, he'll make your wife wish she had never heard of you.'

Grant gave a sudden shiver, and dropped back, silent, unnerved, seeing a mental picture of Christine as she had been at the pool – as she had gone into the bathroom. This woman must surely be able to hear his teeth grating.

After half an hour, the driver pulled into the side of the road, but didn't speak or get out. They waited for five minutes before the chauffeur started off again. Obviously he was making sure he was not being followed. Now he drove faster, and they passed through several small villages and towns.

Rain began to gild the windscreen, and the chauffeur switched on the wipers.

They had been travelling for about an hour when the chauffeur stopped again, this time under a tree. In the headlights Grant could see the white fingers of a signpost, but it was just too far away for him to read the names on it.

Another car pulled up behind them.

Grant leaned forward, tensely.

A man came from the other car and spoke to the chauffeur. The rain still teemed down, and the new-comer's face was hidden by a hat, the brim of which was curled downwards.

'All okay,' this man said. 'You weren't followed.'

'I know I wasn't followed,' said the chauffeur.

'Any trouble?'

'Just like a lamb. He's easy.'

'He'd better be,' said the other. He turned and opened the door. Grant caught a glimpse of the lower part of his face, thick lips and a square chin.

'Come on,' he said. 'You're changing buggies.'

Grant hesitated as rain splashed into the car.

'Don't waste time,' said the girl, quietly, and Grant climbed out.

'Other car,' ordered the man, and the rain was pelting down so heavily that Grant made a dive for it. The door was open, and he climbed into a large limousine, much more luxurious than the first. He turned round to close the door, but someone else, sitting in the corner, closed it for him.

Grant dropped into his corner, and brushed the hair from his eyes. This time, his companion was a man. The driver came back, and the car moved off, as the other car turned in the road and went back the way it had come.

The girl had at least said something.

Grant would not speak first, but he fumbled for his lighter. The figure in the dark corner stretched out a hand, and took the lighter away.

Purgatory could be no worse than this, and memories were like little spiteful demons, stoking the fires of hell.

But before long, the car turned off the road, and Grant saw drive-gates and gate-posts lit up by the headlamps. Then the lights were switched off, the car swung round, gravel grated beneath the wheels as they stopped.

The man in the corner said: 'Out.'

His was a toneless voice, not unlike Carosi's, but it wasn't Carosi's, Grant knew. Something was pressed into his ribs, and he felt a sharp prick of a knife. He climbed out. In front of him was the brooding pile of a huge house. No lights showed at the windows, but he could make out a flight of steps, and a front door. He mounted the steps slowly. There was a wide roof over a porch, giving shelter from the rain.

The man with the knife followed him, after slamming the door. The car moved off to the side of the house as the front door opened.

Grant stepped into a large, dark hall. There was a faint light upstairs, and he could just make out the staircase. 68

He stood stockstill, and the man behind him bumped into him and swore. Grant hardly heard him, the shock was so great. In spite of the gloom, in spite of the fact that he could only just make out the stairs, although he had not recognised the drive-in, *this was his father's house.*

Then bright lights were switched on, dazzling him.

Grant half-closed his eyes, as the man behind him shut the door; he did not see who had opened it. As soon as he could look about him with comfort, he saw the wide sweep of the staircase, everything which was so familiar; this was Grant Manor.

Almost, for the first time, the image of Christine was driven out of his mind; in its place there was his father – Sir Mortimer Grant, once so proud and implacable, telling him of Carosi's blackmail: not broken, but breaking.

'Upstairs,' said the man behind him.

He must keep calm, and keep himself from striking out, must wait. There was so much more at stake: everything; Christine.

He reached the landing, seeing the familiar dark doors all closed, the wide passage which led to the right, towards the servants' wing, the other passages to the main bedrooms and, a door to the left leading to his father's suite: a study, sitting-room, bedroom and bathroom.

'In there,' said the man, and pointed to the door of the suite.

Grant turned to look at him.

He was sharp-faced, and there was a beading of rain on the tip of his nose. He still wore his hat, pushed to the back of his head. His small eyes glinted, and he had a thin ugly mouth.

'You've seen enough,' he said. 'Inside.'

Grant stepped forward and opened the door. The light was on in this room, the sitting-room. No one was there.

The door closed behind him. The key turned in the lock.

Grant pressed his hands against his forehead, trying to push away the nagging ache over his eyes. What was he doing here? How had Carosi managed to gain access, to use it as if it were his own?

There should be whisky, gin, anything he fancied, in the study, which was the next room. The key was in the lock. He had never wanted a drink so much.

The light was on in the study, and he caught his breath. He saw the bookshelves lining three walls from wall to ceiling, the library steps, the deep red carpet, the great walnut desk which stood in the corner ...

And Carosi sitting at his father's desk.

Carosi wore a maroon tuxedo with grey revers. His round sallow face was set in the familiar, apparently meaningless smile. His thick hands were resting on the desk, palms downwards. His narrow eyes were turned towards Grant.

Grant didn't speak, but turned to a cabinet which was built into one of the rows of bookshelves. He opened it with unsteady hands, took out whisky, a syphon and a glass, and poured himself a drink. He drank, turned away from the cabinet, took out his cigarettes, sat down in an easy-chair and lit up.

Then he said: 'Where is my wife?'

'She is safe,' answered Carosi, in his curiously flat voice. 'She is safe for a while.'

'My father?'

'He is now aware that he was wrong to defy me,' said Carosi. 'You will discover the same thing. You made one great mistake, you must not make another.'

Grant said: 'Yes, I made a mistake. I didn't choke the life out of you.'

Carosi lifted his hands, and Grant saw that they had been covering an automatic. 'Don't make another mistake,' he said. 'I am not vindictive any more. You have paid for that. With your wife's help. So charming. I did not understand before. I like her.'

Grant swallowed whisky, and then gripped the arms of his chair. He must not throw his life away, he must wait, wait, wait and listen to this leering brute, this ...

'I like her, very much,' went on Carosi. 'It is perhaps a good thing for her. Perhaps. It may be a good thing for you. I do not know, yet. Grant, I have much to do. No time to waste with you. The past, it is past. I have new plans.'

'Which concern me?' Grant forced himself to ask.

'In some ways, a little, in other ways a great deal.' Carosi spread his thick hands over the gun. 'Grant, I bring you here, I show you I am in possession, your father works with me. He does not do so willingly.'

Grant couldn't keep the question back.

'Is he here?'

'He is here,' said Carosi. A faint sing-song note had crept into his voice. 'He will assist me. You, also. Until you have done what I wish, you will not see your wife again. Your father and your wife are both my hostages. I can ruin your father, easily. Those papers you destroyed, they were but part of the whole story. I have the rest. He does exactly what I require, because he must. No one can help him—or you. You think perhaps of Scotland Yard, that they "protect" you—protect! They allow your wife to be taken away, they cannot save anyone from Carosi. You begin, I hope, to believe that.'

Grant said: 'Yes, I think I do.'

'It is beginning,' approved Carosi. 'Understand this. I am not a mean man. I am big. I forgive you for what you did in the past. But I will make you, all of you, suffer very much if you do not do what I tell you in future. That is understood?'

Grant felt suffocatingly hot. 'Yes.'

'It must be. I shall watch you, closely. In my life I learn one big rule. I trust no one. But of the police. Through you, they hope, they catch Carosi. So, I make big trouble.' He laughed. 'They concentrate near Uplands. Good! You will return there, and wait until you have instructions from me how to behave. You will be attacked. Often. You will not be killed, you will not be hurt. You understand?'

Grant said: 'I think so.'

'It is what they call the decoy,' Carosi said. 'You will appear very frightened. Worried, for your wife. You will always complain bitterly. You will do all you can to make it appear you are afraid of being killed. But if you behave as I instruct you, you will be all right.'

Grant said: 'I don't get it.'

'I will also tell you this,' said Carosi. 'You fail me, you disobey, and many unpleasant things happen to your wife. Tell the police you have come to a house where you are told you will find her. She is not there, so you return to Uplands. Then wait. I will send instructions.'

'You didn't bring me here just to tell me that and send me back.'

'No, no,' said Carosi. 'I bring you here to show you that I have much power. I possess your father's house. It is one place where the police will not consider looking. I repeat: you will receive instructions about what to do from time to time. That is all.'

Sweat was standing out on Grant's forehead, and his voice grated.

'I'll do what you want, but let me—let me see my wife.'

'No. She will remain all right, if you obey. But wait.' Carosi put out a hand, touched a bell-push, and sat back, putting his hands over the gun again. Grant hardly knew how to sit there, not knowing what to expect, not daring to hope, but hoping. Then footsteps sounded in the outer room, and the door opened.

Grant saw his father.

Chapter Twelve

Betrayal

Sir Mortimer entered the study quietly and closed the door. He nodded to Carosi, then looked at his son. He was tall and imposing, rather florid of face and running to fat. His eyes were grey – the same colour as his son's – and he was strangely calm.

Grant saw the lines at his forehead and the mouth, of great cares and anxiety. His father walked heavily, too, with none of the once familiar buoyancy.

'Well, Michael,' he said, very quietly.

Grant said: 'Hello, Dad,' in an empty voice.

'I have told your son the position,' said Carosi. 'You will confirm it, please. Be brief.'

'Yes, all right,' said Sir Mortimer. 'Mike—I'm desperately sorry. The truth is that Carosi carries too many guns for me, For you, too. We must let him have his own way.'

'Just what has happened?' asked Grant, and there was bitterness in his voice.

'Simply that I know I can't fight any longer,' said his father. 'I'm too old to fight now. After the last affair, I thought all would be well. I didn't know how strong a hold Carosi had. I have been taking his instructions for over a year.'

'I see,' said Mike heavily.

A year, and he hadn't known; a year, and he had thought himself such a hero, so much smarter than the police, while Carosi had so frightened his father that this had been kept from him.

'You will have to do the same,' said Sir Mortimer. 'He is quite capable of doing anything to Christine.'

'I think that is enough,' interrupted Carosi. 'You will go, Sir Mortimer, please. And Grant, if I am caught before my work is finished, you will not see your wife again.'

The tragedy for Grant was that his father turned and left the room as if he were a humble servant.

Grant had never hated a man as he hated Carosi.

'You will go back to Uplands now,' said Carosi. 'Remember to tell the police that this has been a wild-goose chase—you found no one at the end of it. You will be taken to Croydon, from there you will return to Uplands as you wish. Good night'

'Good night,' Grant made himself respond.

He went out, feeling as old as his father.

He crossed the empty sitting-room, hesitated by the door, and looked round as if expecting to find that this was a mirage.

The door was unlocked. He went out on to the landing, and the thin-faced man who had driven him here stood at the foot of the stairs, beckoning. But it was impossible for Grant to hurry; the vision of his father, the numb helplessness in that voice, and the realization of the futility of his own actions, all combined to affect him. His legs seemed stiff, his feet leaden. He had gone storming into Carosi's flat – and condemned his father to servility, damned Christine to – what?

Was she in this house?

He knew that even if she was, he dare not try to find her. Carosi had made sure of that.

What evil genius sparked the man, to give him such ample power?

'Get a move on,' the other man said, opening the front door. 'Stopped raining, that's one good thing. I—'

He broke off, and something like a scream started in his throat. It did not come out. Grant saw a man's dark figure dart forward from the side of the porch. Next moment, the driver was slithering down, silent, helpless. His feet kicked against Grant, who backed away. The light streamed out of the hall on to the rain-soaked drive, where puddles glistened.

The man who had attacked the driver said almost conversationally: 'Is Carosi here, Grant?'

The voice was West's, of Scotland Yard. But he was dark-haired and had a dark moustache and looked much older.

Three other men came out of the shadows, and stepped swiftly into the porch. Police. Two slipped past Grant as West took his arm and pushed him into the hall. That attack had been frightening in its silent speed.

'Is he here?' demanded West again, and now Grant recognised his eyes.

'He—yes, but—' Fear because of Carosi's threats welled up in Grant, and stifled his words. If Carosi thought he had plotted this with the police ...

He did not realise how remarkable it was that he did not take it for granted that Carosi would be caught tonight.

'Where is he?' West demanded urgently.

'Upstairs. West! There's something I must tell you.'

'Keep it,' said West. 'Stay here.' He slipped out into the porch again, and Grant heard him whisper. A moment later an engine started up, and a car moved down the drive.

West came back.

'Better let them think you've gone,' he said. 'How many people are there about; do you know?'

'I—I've only seen two,' said Grant. 'West, my wife—'

'If she's here we'll get her,' West said. 'Don't worry, Grant.'

'If Carosi thinks I planned this, he'll kill her.'

'If he's got any sense, he'll know we had police in cars, on bicycles and on foot keeping a look-out for you, and were in touch by radio nearly all the time,' West said. 'I was on the train from Salisbury, too.

We've a dozen men, some at the back, some at the drive-gates, some on each side. Carosi hasn't a chance!'

Had Christine?

If Grant joined with West now, if Carosi got away, if Christine wasn't here …

The thoughts and fears made anguish in Grant's mind, and suddenly, wildly, he hated this policeman, with his damnable calm and cocksureness, for West might be passing sentence of death on Christine.

He mustn't let West get Carosi.

'Where was Carosi?' West asked. 'The quicker it's over the better, now.'

Now that he had made up his mind, Grant felt much easier.

'He was in my room,' he lied. 'Upstairs, along the first wide passage, and it's the second door on the left.'

'In *your* room?' West looked startled.

'This is my father's house.'

'Good Lord!' said West. 'That's hard.' Damn him for the compassion in his voice. 'Lead the way, will you?'

Grant said: 'West, I've had a hell of a time, and I'm all in.'

Now he needed that compassion.

'All right, stay there,' said West, and raised his voice just loud enough to be heard in the hall. 'Follow me, you two.'

Grant waited until they had disappeared at the head of the stairs, then hurried after them, the carpet muffling the sound. Their backs were towards him when he entered the sitting-room, crossed to the study, and opened the door. Carosi was standing by one of the book-lined walls.

'Grant, why are you here?' His voice was still hoarse and unflurried. 'I told you that—'

'West is here, and has men all round,' Grant said. 'If you're to get away, you'll have to use the side door. Go through—'

'I know the way,' interrupted Carosi, and gave a smile that was surprisingly human as he added: 'You will be well rewarded for this.'

* * *

Roger West went up those stairs with a vigour and eagerness which matched his mood. They'd catch Carosi. He had staked everything on this one throw, and could afford to pat himself on the back for anticipating what train Grant would catch, for getting some theatrical make-up from the hotel, borrowing an old suit from Fratton, making-up on the train. Fleet Street would give this banner headlines.

'Yard Man, Disguised, Catches Carosi!'

He felt a fierce excitement as he tried the handle of the door, and then felt it yield. The other men were poised and ready.

West flung the door back, on to an empty room.

Half an hour later, he gave up the search.

At half past ten next morning, Roger entered Scotland Yard, and found a kind of furtive interest everywhere – among the men on duty in the main hall, in the uniformed and plainclothes officers, and especially in Eddie Day. Eddie was alone in the office.

'Been having quite a time, haven't you?' he asked, sitting back to relish this. 'I told you so, 'Andsome—you ought to 'ave—*have*—put Carosi away months ago. Years ago, if it comes to that.'

'You didn't tell me how,' said Roger, and lifted the telephone and asked for Chatworth.

'Come right away,' Chatworth said. No headmaster could have sounded more forbidding.

'Don't go for a minute,' pleaded Eddie. 'Tell me what happened last night.'

'Eddie,' said Roger, patiently, 'it'll be in the papers. Why don't you treat yourself to one?'

Chatworth sat like a prosperous farmer behind his shiny desk. He nodded and pointed to a chair.

'I feel like hell about this,' Roger said.

'I know how you feel,' growled Chatworth. 'And I know you didn't have the luck. How much did you miss Carosi by?'

'Minutes, at most. He'd been in a different room, the chair he'd been sitting on was still warm, and his prints were on a brandy glass that was warm, too. Grant gave him his chance, of course. There's a side entrance from the suite; it used to be the way the Lord of the Manor's light o' love sneaked in and out.'

Chatworth said: 'Any sign of Mrs Grant?'

'No, none at all. She certainly hadn't been held there. I'd say Grant warned Carosi in order to give his wife a chance. I'm beginning to get an obsession about Carosi, sir.'

'Meaning what?'

'That he's bigger and better than we know, and that he's got a stranglehold on a good many people in high positions. Obviously, Sir Mortimer Grant is under his thumb again. He says that Carosi held him there under duress, but I'll put my money on Sir Mortimer having worked with Carosi. All the regular staff have been dismissed, for instance. Sir Mortimer says he's going away, but—' Roger broke off. 'We did pick up a bit at the house, though. Carosi had left a file of papers behind. In it were letters from three other men we think have been blackmailed.'

'Who?'

'Lord Raffety, Sir Arnold Dana, and Wilfred Harrison.'

'My God!' breathed Chatworth. 'About fifty million pounds' worth of men!'

'That's what I estimated,' Roger said, quietly. 'I want to talk to each one, sir.'

'Go ahead,' Chatworth said, and he looked positively shaken. 'What do you think Carosi's after? Any idea at all?'

'I wouldn't like to make a guess,' Roger said, 'but we can count it in millions, sir. And we can also count it in terms of human misery.'

'Get Carosi, Roger,' Chatworth said quietly. 'I'll back you with everything I've got.'

Not one of the three millionaires admitted knowing Carosi.

None of Carosi's known associates turned up.

Grant stayed at Uplands, like a brooding bear. Sir Mortimer did not go away, but lived almost like a hermit in his country home.

There was no trace of Christine Grant.

Nothing gave Roger any hope until Arthur Morely, her father, was reported to be staying in a Kentish seaside town.

'You'll go down at once, won't you?' Chatworth said to Roger, when the report came in.

'Yes, as soon as I can,' Roger said, and went on very quietly: 'I think it's a bait, of course. Carosi must know that we know Morely was his go-between with Grant, and he's allowed Morely to show up simply because it suits him.'

'Well?'

Roger said: 'I think it's a bait, then, and that it would be a good thing to swallow it. We haven't a line on Carosi. We only know that he's the biggest powder-keg in the country. If he can force men like Mortimer, Dana, Raffety and the others to do what he wants, there's no knowing how widespread his influence it. We've got to find out. So I've got to swallow that bait, and hope that Carosi himself is holding the other end.'

Chatworth said gruffly: 'If ever Carosi gets hold of you, Roger, he might not let you go. You've hounded him more than any man alive. And you've a wife and children. Remember?'

Roger's eyes were expressionless.

'I'd like permission to swallow that bait, sir.'

There was a long pause. Then: 'Handle the job as you feel wise,' Chatworth said.

Chapter Thirteen

Bait

Morely sat on a seat overlooking the English Channel, smoking a cigarette and sunning himself. He looked much healthier than he had at Salisbury, and more prosperous too. There was a gentle smile on his face, as if he were dreaming of pleasant things.

Roger passed him twice, then went and sat down beside him. Morely glanced round, and murmured that it was a nice day.

'Very,' said Roger. He wore a pair of baggy flannels, one knee of which was patched, a pullover and an old sports coat. His hair was dyed again, and he had put on a heavy moustache, but it would deceive no one by day. It was intended to look like a disguise, not to be one.

Three navvies, working at a hole in the road, fifty yards along, were Yard men: if Carosi was up to form, he would know that, and would assume that the police were hoping to make a capture. He would not dream that Roger was offering himself as a kind of sacrifice.

Give Carosi's men half a chance, and they would kidnap him.

Morely showed no sign of recognition, but seemed to doze, then kept glancing at an old gun metal watch which he had on a steel chain. It was nearly half past eleven. At half past exactly, he stood up and sauntered along the promenade. There were low cliffs here, and at intervals, shallow steps which led down to the beach. Not far along was a boating station, with a dozen rowing-boats, one or two small yachts, pedal boats, canoes and motor-boats for hire. It was early in the season, and few people were about.

Roger followed Morely.

Christine Grant's father might just be out for a stroll, but Roger could not bring himself to believe it; there must be more significance in it than that.

The browny yellow sand was very fine. A few small children played in it. A girl with a wide sun hat and wearing a sleeveless white dress which seemed to show every curve of her body came walking along with a great Alsatian dog behind her; it was now sniffing, now loping.

Roger's heart began to thump with physical fear.

A dog like this had savaged and killed young Derek Allen. A dog like this could leap at him and catch him by the throat.

The policemen navvies had knocked off for their tea-break, because he had left the seat; but they were some distance away.

The girl was a beauty, and the dog was a beauty, too.

Then Michael Grant came striding from the other direction. He was in grey flannels and blue reefer jacket, head bare, eyes scanning first the distant sea and then the girl and Roger. It wasn't an accident that they had met close to the little jetties, where motor-boats were moored. The girl had not even looked at Roger, but was smiling at Grant, as if with warm welcome. The dog came bounding up, and Roger instinctively put a hand up towards his throat, had to force himself not to back away.

'You won't get hurt, West,' said Grant, 'if you'll come for a boat trip with us.'

'What on earth do you mean?' Roger gasped. 'My name is Simpson; I—'

'Don't try it on,' Grant said flatly. 'If you do, this lovely will give a signal to the dog, and all those shovel-plying coppers on the promenade won't be able to help you. Just go and get into that boat called *New Day,* the newly varnished one.'

The girl was smiling, a soft and gentle smile; she looked far too sweet and pure to be evil. But she held a hand towards the dog, as if a command; and the dog was looking up at Roger, great head on one side.

Morely was some way off, still walking steadily away.

'Listen, West,' Grant said almost desperately, 'I mean what I say. Carosi wants to see you, and nothing will stop him. If you've got any sense you'll come with us now. If you don't, the next thing you'll know he'll be after your wife or the children.'

'He *loves* children,' cooed the girl, with another sugary smile. 'Do come with us. Mr West, I'm sure a boat trip will do you a world of good. And a friend of yours would like to see you, too—a Mr Fingleton, of the *Monitor*. He *is* a friend of yours, isn't he? He tried to harass Mr Carosi, and it didn't work out quite as he expected it.'

'West—' Grant began.

There was a sudden squeal of brakes on the road above.

Roger swung round. A car was swinging off the road and mounting the pavement. One of the policemen was on the ground, and the other two were pinned against the railings. The timing was perfect; even if he had wanted help he would not have had a chance.

'Come on,' Grant rasped. 'Get moving.'

The dog growled.

'If you kill a policeman,' Roger began, as if he were fighting back naked fear, 'every man in the force will be after you, and—'

'I'm sure that will frighten Mr Carosi ever so much,' the girl said.

They were well out to sea. It was calm, and it could have been pleasant. The dog lay in the thwarts, and the girl dangled one arm gracefully over the side so that the water rippled through her fingers. Not far off, a motor cruiser of some fifty or sixty tons was hove to, and they were heading for it. The gangway was already down.

Was he going to see Carosi now? Was this how the man kept away from the police, by cruising outside territorial waters?

They drew alongside. A sailor in snow-white clothes was standing by to help them aboard.

'You first,' the girl said, and smiled at him, and Roger climbed on to the bottom step with his back to the land and to all he held dear;

he went up. The cruiser seemed much larger now, and spick and span. Two more men in white were at the top of the gangway, and one gave him a hand.

He didn't need help. He just wanted to see Carosi.

He did not see Carosi at once, he saw Fingleton.

The reporter looked like a man who had been through an ordeal beyond words. It showed in his eyes, at his lips, in the bruises on his face. He seemed hardly to recognise Roger as he sat in a small, dark cabin, until Roger schooled himself to ask: 'What happened to you, Fingleton?'

'The great newspaper man,' Fingleton said bitterly. 'The Fleet Street ace who was going to out-Yard the Yard, and out-glamour West. I thought I was on to something. I traced a line between Carosi and Lord Raffety. I went to see Raffety—and when I came away, I walked into a reception party. Mr Carosi wanted me to tell him exactly how I found the line to Raffety. I wouldn't. But I think I will, West. That man is—'

He broke off, and there was fear in his eyes.

The door was locked, but before long a man came in with a tray and some food, and Fingleton fell upon the food as if he hadn't eaten for days.

Roger made himself eat a little.

Within twenty minutes he realised that had been a mistake, for he began to feel overwhelmingly drowsy.

The food had been drugged, of course, and only one question burned in his mind.

Was it enough to kill?

When he came round, someone not far off was laughing. It was gusty laughter, as of a man doubled up with mirth, and yet with a different note in it – as if the laugh *hurt* the man. Wherever he looked, there was only darkness, but a light showed under the door, and peal after peal of tortured merriment came, as if the man could not help himself.

Roger got up from a chair. He swayed, and his head hammered, while that awful, hysterical laughter grated in his mind, killing all desire to think.

He reached the door.

By then he was bathed in sweat, his legs felt weak, and he was afraid that he was going to fall. But he groped for the handle, and found it.

The door opened when he pushed. He waited for a few seconds, to get used to the light, then thrust the door wider open, and stepped into the room beyond.

It was empty.

Another peal of laughter rang out from another room beyond. He went towards it. This one was in a house – a sitting-room. So he was ashore again. He looked back into the room from which he had come, and saw a bed.

The laughter died away into a giggling sound – strange, frightening giggling. Roger went forward to the next door, and opened it on another wild burst of laughter.

Fingleton was spread-eagled on a single bed in the corner of a small room. He was naked, except for his small trunks. Every bruise showed. Sitting on a stool at the foot was a girl, casually tickling Fingleton's feet with a long feather. The girl of the beach and the floppy hat, and the dog. She wasn't smiling, but looked bored; that made it more horrible. She didn't seem to realise that Roger had entered the room. She stopped tickling, and Fingleton gave a little convulsive shudder and stopped laughing. But he didn't lie still. His chest heaved, he gasped for breath, Roger could hear it whistling through his mouth and nose. He was running with sweat – down his face, his forehead, his chest, his legs and arms. Now that he wasn't laughing, he looked as if he were writhing in agony; in fact he was.

The girl moved the feather and touched the sole of Fingleton's right foot, just as the reporter had seemed to get a little repose.

Fingleton heaved.

Roger went forward, snatched the feather from her, crumpled it up in his hand, and flung it away.

The girl wasn't really surprised, but she looked round at him blankly, reproachfully.

'You mustn't do that,' she protested. 'Mr Carosi will be cross.'

She sounded almost simple, and did not speak or protest when Roger went to the bed, feeling in his hip pocket for his knife – but it wasn't there. His keys were, as well as some odd silver. Fingleton looked up at him without recognition. His eyes were bloodshot and pain-racked. His tongue showed as he muttered a word: *water*. There was no water in the room, no taps, no hand-basin. There might be a hand-basin in the other bedroom, though. The girl hadn't got the feather now.

'Don't touch him again,' he growled, and turned and went into the sitting-room, then across to the bedroom. There was a hand-basin, with a tooth-glass on the rack above it; there was a sponge too. He ran cold water on to the sponge, squeezed it nearly dry, soaked it again, and then filled the glass and turned round.

Fingleton began to laugh again!

'Stop it!' shouted Roger. 'Stop it!' He rushed into the sitting-room, seeing the girl sitting in exactly the same position, with another long quill in her hand. He reached the door, but she slammed it in his face.

Water spilled over the edge of the glass as he tried to open it, while Fingleton went on laughing, those maniacal sounds which seemed so horrible.

Roger turned to put the glass down, to hurl his weight against the wood.

'You seem very concerned about your friend,' said Carosi, from the door behind him.

Roger lowered the glass and the sponge, as Fingleton's laughter died away. He turned round, slowly. Carosi backed to a chair in the sitting-room. He was smiling what Christine Grant had called a Chinaman's smile.

'Fingleton will not laugh again, if you tell me the truth,' Carosi said in that voice which sounded as if he was recovering from a cold. 'Put those things down, West, and sit down opposite me.'

Silence came from the room beyond.

Roger carried the glass and sponge to a small table, put them down and dropped into the chair and looked at Carosi. He tried to tell himself that he was not afraid, but he was.

'I have seen you like this before,' Carosi said, evenly, 'although you perhaps did not realise it. The disguise—' He raised his hands, and Roger saw that he held an automatic. 'It would serve once, perhaps, if a man were not able to see beyond it. Very simple. You are a simple man, West. You have simple rules. One thing is right, another is wrong. You are always on the side of the right. But life is not as simple as that. You are a victim of a false culture and a false civilization. You are kind. Nature is cruel. Man is natural. I want a thing. I take it. A man opposes me. I make him suffer. A man refuses to tell me the truth. He is tortured until he does. Simple also in its own way, perhaps—but natural.'

Roger didn't speak; was glad even of this slight respite.

'And you have the faults of this veneer of civilization,' went on Carosi. 'You suffer because another man is in agony. That is bad. I do not suffer. I hardly notice it. I train others not to notice it. I always find that the strongest weapon to use is that which plays on another's emotions and affections. Grant, and his wife. You, and your wife and family perhaps—and Fingleton. But you carry it too far; Fingleton does not matter to you. What do you think of me, Chief Inspector West?'

Roger didn't answer, because he could not: there was nothing to say. Then Carosi gave a short sharp whistle, and almost at once *Fingleton began to laugh!*

Roger started up. 'You told me—'

'I keep my promises,' said Carosi. 'You will learn that. You refused to answer my question. What do you think of me? Will you answer now?'

Fingleton's laughter died away.

'Yes,' said Roger, hoarsely. 'I'll answer you, I think—'

He paused.

'Be quite frank,' urged Carosi. 'You will find that we have things in common, West. For instance, I like the truth.'

Roger said: 'I don't think I know what I think. I did know. This has altered my opinion.'

'For better or worse?'

'Worse.'

'That is the truth. Good,' said Carosi. 'What did you think about me before, West? I was just an important criminal—as you would say. Yes?'

'Yes.'

'Let me know, please, exactly what you thought of my methods, my activities—everything,' said Carosi. 'You will understand that I seldom have the chance to discuss this with a police officer.' This was a game he wanted to play: so why not humour him? It should be easy, but – there was that steady gaze from the narrowed eyes, giving Roger a feeling, almost a fear that if he lied, Carosi would know.

'It isn't easy to sum up what I thought,' he said. 'Are you clever? Up to a point. Clever enough to get what you want, to make people faithful to you, to make a lot of money, even clever enough to leave the country when things got too hot. But not really clever enough. I was sure you would come back. Whenever a man becomes as powerful as you, he can't keep away from the source of his power. If you were really clever, you wouldn't have come back.'

'A matter of opinion,' said Carosi. 'And what else? Please.'

'That you were as bad as men are made,' Roger said. 'That you enjoy watching pain, in causing pain for the sake of watching it, you get pleasure out of seeing and hearing a man in agony.'

'Oh no,' protested Carosi calmly. 'That is not true. I get no pleasure out of hurting your friend Fingleton. It just does not matter. If I could get all I want without it, I would not trouble to cause any man or woman pain, but sometimes it is the only way. But to get pleasure—no. I simply do not care. Tell me, you regard me as different from the ordinary criminal? The thief. The man, like Arthur Morely, who becomes jealous and murders his wife. You would not consider I was the same as them?'

'No,' said Roger, 'not now.'

'Why not, please?'

'They know they're doing wrong when they do it,' Roger said very carefully. 'They know the difference between right and wrong, they do a thing and take the consequences. You don't. You take a pretty girl and ruin her life, and—'

'That is the sentiment,' interrupted Carosi. 'I have no time for that, none at all. I have affection for some people—like Julieta. She is in the other room. And like Christine Grant. I find her charming. I like her beauty. Yes, I like loveliness; to possess; to use. Julieta—you do not know the story of Julieta, perhaps.'

Roger said helplessly: 'No.'

'She was a child when I first knew her,' Carosi told him. 'Of Spanish parents. Good to look at perhaps, but not beautiful like she is now. Young and promising. I thought, one day you will be just right for my bed. But she had a mind as well as a body. I did not make her into one of the girls to send away. She is just another *mind*. I have a great doctor, who helped me to train her, to cure her of what you call emotion. She does what she is told, always, without arguing. Good—bad? The only good thing is what I say, the only bad thing is what I dislike. That is Julieta. It was an experiment, as you would say. It has been one of my great successes.'

'It could prove to be your greatest crime,' said Roger, and then realised that this man meant exactly what he said. 'To corrupt and break—'

'No, no, no!' exclaimed Carosi. 'Understand me, West. She has one code of what you call morals, you have another. They are different, that is all. You were trained to do "good" things—on a certain code. She on another. You have loyalty to your employers. She to me. She is content. She has everything she could want. Her dogs, too—the affection you would perhaps have her give to a man, she gives to them. It is an outlet, a safety-valve. Those who work for me always have a safety-valve, West. They are sent away for a few weeks to do exactly what they like. I have just sent away a number of them from London, those for whom you have been looking. They have a rest. And they will come back when I require them. Now—did you understand before what I was like?'

Roger said thickly: 'No.'

'Then, perhaps, you will admit how wrong you were in some of your judgements,' Carosi said. He shifted his position. 'Good—that is the first part. The second need not take long. How much have you learned about what I am going to do?'

Roger could tell the simple truth, but would Carosi believe it?

The door opened as Carosi spoke, and the girl Julieta entered the room.

She wore a close-fitting housecoat of wine-red silk; it was very full-skirted, and billowed out as she moved across the room and sat down on a pouf.

'How are you getting on?' she asked, and gave her sugary smile.

'So far, very well,' said Carosi, complacently. 'I congratulate you, Julieta; you told me that West would not lie to me about myself. He has been very frank. Now, we come to different business – I wish to know what he has learned about my future plans. Well, West? What have you learned?'

The matter-of-factness in his manner did nothing to help. He was deadly, and he had no scruples, no feelings at all. Roger could sense that: knew now why dealing with Carosi had been so different and so difficult.

'I don't know a thing,' he said.

Carosi's smile faded slowly, and it was remarkable that Roger should feel his nerves becoming taut again, and feel the dullness of fear. But it was so.

'West,' said Carosi, 'you must not lie to me. I can always tell when a man lies. Fingleton lied. He visited one of my -associates. He must have had a reason, but he says not. I do not want to be unpleasant, West.'

Julieta said smilingly: 'Of course you don't, but if Mr West should be so silly—' She took an envelope out of her pocket and extracted a card. 'He will have only himself to blame if anything happens to—'

She turned the card over.

This was a photograph of his wife and two sons.

'West,' asked Carosi, 'what do you know of my future plans?'

'I don't know a tiling,' Roger said, hard-voiced. 'I know that you've got Sir Mortimer Grant, Lord Raffety, Sir Arnold Dana and Wilfred Harrison under your thumb. None will admit it, let alone tell me how, or what you're making them do. If I know these four, I assume there are many more, and—'

'You *guess?*'

'That's as far as I've got.'

'What a very good guess you have made!' said Carosi. 'Hasn't he, Julieta? Take him back to his friend Fingleton, my dear.'

Chapter Fourteen

Man Alone

Fingleton was asleep on the bed, no longer spread-eagled and tied down. Someone had washed his face. The pillow-case was snowy white, so was the part of the sheet in sight. The contrast between this and what Roger had seen before seemed part and parcel of the plot to keep his nerves at an agonizing stretch.

Carosi as a man was the frightening, fearsome factor. The flat, hoarse voice, the trick of motionlessness, the way of demonstrating just what power he had, of hinting at what he could do, to – anyone.

To millionaires.

To Janet and the boys.

It was easy to understand why Grant had submitted, now, why he was helping Carosi. It was hard to believe that anyone could defy him.

He, Roger West, bright boy of the Yard, was obsessed by Carosi's nature, could think of little else. He ought to be scheming to get out of this room, of searching this house, of getting away with whatever he found, but he wasn't: it was as if Carosi had put a steel band round his mind.

He had to break it.

He had to use this chance, probably the last he would ever have.

Fingleton might help.

Grant might …

It was wishful thinking, Roger knew: whatever he did would have to be done on his own.

He went to the window and pulled the curtains back, seeing the moonlight night.

The window wasn't barred or locked, as Carosi did not think there was much chance for him to escape.

The soft moon shone upon a lovely countryside. He could distinguish huge, spreading trees in a great park. Not far away was a compound, and dogs were leaping and howling frenziedly. He could make out the iron fence and the three men who were standing just outside the compound. They had two of the dogs with them. One of the men locked the gate, then the three men and the two dogs walked away out of sight.

Escape would be suicide.

Cautiously, Roger opened the window, and as he did so, heard a man and a woman talking.

The man was Michael Grant.

The woman—?

Grant did not know where he was either.

He had done exactly what he had been told, because of what might happen if he refused. He was haunted by the sight of his father's slow, weary movements and his hopelessness, and he could not get Christine out of his mind, for more than a few minutes on end. He had been promised that he would see her if he helped with West; and he had helped. He felt out of his mind because of that betrayal, because of his fears.

He had prayed that he would see Christine on board the motor cruiser, but he had been taken to a cabin, told he would be there for some hours, and eaten the meal brought in to him.

He had slept afterwards, realising only in the last few minutes of waking that he had been drugged. Frantically he had tried to fight the effect off, but failed.

He woke in darkness.

He did not know how long he had been unconscious, and had no idea where he was, except that he was not at sea. Then after a while he realised that someone else was in the room, breathing softly.

West?

He lay for a while in the darkness, then stretched out a hand, groped, found a bedside lamp, and switched it on.

Asleep in the bed next to him was Christine. Christine!

Soon, she woke ...

After the first few minutes of incoherent delight, they began to talk, swift, almost incoherent words. Grant could not keep his gaze away from his wife's face; Christine had recaptured something of the radiance of her wedding day. The fact that they both were Carosi's prisoners did not seem to matter.

They talked about everything that had happened, and then about West; and Roger West heard them, in this country house that was also a prison.

Next morning, Roger saw the Grants being driven off in a dark limousine. The gracious parkland seemed to swallow them up, and they disappeared. He could not be sure that this was England, but believed it was. He knew that he would have to do nothing today, unless an unexpected chance offered itself: all he could do was to wait for a chance.

A timid woman who was raddled and made-up absurdly, brought him breakfast. An hour afterwards, Julieta came to invite him to go out with her. She meant it. He went out of the bedroom on to a wide landing, down a spacious staircase, into a noble hall. It was in England, there seemed no longer doubt of that.

Soon Julieta walked with him across the springy turf, glancing up now and again. They were halfway between a huge Georgian house and a ring of trees which hemmed in the parkland. She wore the white sleeveless dress, with its curious mixture of purity and voluptuousness, but no hat.

In front of them, two Alsatians walked with heads well up, sniffing the air, seldom running far away.

The other dogs were in a yard behind the house.

They drew very near the ring of trees.

There was a lot of thick undergrowth, surprising for so early in the summer, and Roger could not see far. But beyond the trees was the outside world. He wondered what would happen now if he called out for help, or lost his head and made a run for the trees. Then he glanced at the dogs, which were so friendly and affectionate to Julieta.

'I don't think we will go any farther,' said Julieta, with her strange simplicity. 'Are you enjoying it?'

'Very much.'

'It seemed a pity to keep you locked up for so long,' said Julieta, 'and you cannot do harm. You are very closely watched, of course. There are men among the trees, and if there were any alarm, more dogs would be released. I hope you will do nothing silly.'

'Not here and now, anyhow,' Roger said. 'It's a lovely spot.' He turned and looked at the house, and murmured, 'It's the first time I've ever realised what was meant by the phrase, the stately homes of England. Glorious, isn't it?'

Julieta laughed.

'Yes, but *is* it England? No, do not answer! It is time to go back.'

When they were near the house, Carosi had appeared on the front steps. Although he was some distance away, it was easy to identify his squat figure.

'Carosi's kingdom,' Roger said, almost casually.

Julieta laughed.

'How right that is! And how much it would please Carosi just to hear you say that. Do you know that he has taken a liking to you, Mr West?'

'Has he?' Roger fought back the savage comment which came to his lips. 'How much good will that do me?'

'Perhaps very much,' said Julieta, brightly. 'Now you are a poor man, but with Carosi, you could become rich. Be friendly with him, please. The day might come when you will be glad of that.'

The day might come when he would strangle Carosi with his bare hands, if he had no other choice.

Julieta was looking at him with those deceptively smiling eyes. She hadn't a mind of her own, remember; she was just a reflection of Carosi's mind.

'He is not all what you think,' she declared simply. 'He tells you the truth. Michael Grant has done what Carosi wanted, so he has been allowed to go home, with his wife.'

Roger stopped in the middle of a pace.

'What?'

'Oh, but it is true. Also, the newspaper man Fingleton became sensible. He told us that he had followed a man who once worked for Carosi to Lord Raffety's house. That was last week. He convinced Carosi that he knows no more, so he has gone, also. Carosi does not kill for the sake of it. And now, he has taken a liking to you. He would like you to work with him. He will watch and, perhaps soon, offer that chance to you. But if you should say yes, and then betray him, he would have no mercy. He would have no mercy at all.'

She smiled so sweetly.

Roger said: 'If he's such a humanitarian, why did he set that dog on to Grant?'

'Oh, not on to Grant,' said Julieta, and her smile was charming as she turned to face him. 'On to the boy who was at that hotel. Michael Grant was in no danger. Carosi simply wished for help. The boy was killed, and Grant was brought to heel. You see?'

Roger said in a grating voice: 'What you mean is that Carosi was afraid that Michael Grant could spoil his plans, so a helpless youth who knew nothing about it at all was murdered to make an example.'

'Yes,' said Julieta, frankly. 'That is why Carosi always gets his way. He is so thorough.'

There seemed few people in the house.

Roger was not locked in his room, and was allowed to go wherever he liked. He had a sense of being watched, but there was no outward evidence of it. There seemed a likelihood that Julieta was right, and that Carosi would like him as a new recruit. There was even a possibility that if he did get an offer, and accepted, he might find out enough to betray the man.

Dare he?

Dare he even think about it?

It was on the third day there, when he was in a library with Carosi, that Carosi was called away. Roger was left alone. He sensed now that he was being even more closely watched, that Carosi expected him to start searching, to take what looked like a heaven-sent chance. So he sat in his chair, smoking, waiting; for ten minutes, for twenty, for half an hour.

There was a file on the desk, with papers in it, a file he could easily reach. The temptation was almost overwhelming, but he fought it back.

When Carosi came in, he was smiling.

'It is well, that was good news,' he said. 'It will not be very long, and I think that all I wish will come about.' He was fingering a small disc, red on one side and with some lettering on the other. He put it on the desk, and soon afterwards a man whom Roger had not seen before came in and said: 'Did you keep my pass, sir?'

Carosi said: 'You dropped it from your wallet. That was very careless.'

He looked steadily at the man, and Roger saw fear draining the colour from the other's face. The man did not move, just stared into Carosi's eyes.

'Do not do that again,' Carosi said, and held up the disc. The man came forward for it, as if he were afraid of what would happen if he got too near.

Nothing happened.

Carosi let the man take the disc.

But when he left he was badly frightened.

A disc, red on one side, with lettering on the other, was a 'pass'. About the size of half a crown, quite ordinary-looking, it was rather like the badge that members of a conference pinned to their coat lapel for easy identification.

That was one thing learned.

It seemed the only thing, until Carosi said on that same evening: 'It will not be long before I have furnished this work in England, West, and after that perhaps we shall come to understand each other. Yes?'

'We might,' Roger said, as if he meant it, and Julieta murmured her approval.

But from that moment on, all he could think of was getting out of here; of warning the Yard that the climax was near. He did not think that Carosi was lying, because Carosi did not lie. He had no more idea what lay behind in the man's mind than he had before. That was the bitter truth.

He had to get out now, although the effort to work from within had failed.

Yet the armed men and the dogs guarded the grounds day and night, unceasingly.

For the rest of that day, in his bedroom, Roger brooded over the position. Sooner or later he would have to make a break. If he could find out for certain where this house was, it might help.

Supposing he couldn't get out.

He thrust that out of his mind, but from then on another factor nagged at his mind.

Was there any chance of the Yard finding *him*?

Did they know that Grant was free? Could Fingleton help?

The sense of being forgotten, left to fend for himself, was very sharp.

He awakened late, feeling tired and jaded; the sleep had done him little good. Maisie, the middle-aged, forlorn-looking maid, came into his room.

'Hallo, dearie,' she said, mechanically. 'Time to get up! Going to be all right for today, anyhow.'

'Why?' snapped Roger.

'Why, me old cock-sparrow? The boss 'as gone out for the day. Taken that female piece of flint with him, too. I don't mind Carosi so much, but that girl, I'd like to—'

Words seldom failed Maisie.

Roger said: 'Maisie, have you ever tried to get out of this place?'

'They don't keep me locked up all the time,' said Maisie, 'they trust *me*. I have a look at the lakes sometimes, and have a day in Dub—'

She broke off, biting her tongue.

Roger covered his surge of hope with a yawn.

'So there are some lakes near here, are there? Westmorland, I suppose?'

'Never *you* mind,' said Maisie. 'I never ought to have said so much. Just you keep your mouth shut, Mr West. I don't mind telling you that the guards have got orders to kill you if you try to get away. And they'd do it.'

She flounced out of the room.

Roger sat up, forgetful of everything she had said, except the significant sentence she hadn't quite completed: Where had she meant but Dublin?

And the lakes of Killarney!

He was thinking of that, and feeling fierce excitement, when he heard several of the dogs barking. He went to the window, and saw five of them, leaping about, and saw two armed men with them.

He needed no telling: this was an alarm.

Were the police here?

Chapter Fifteen

Kinara

Roger stood at the window of his room, tense and rigid, watching the men and the dogs in the grounds, the dogs barking and snarling, the men carrying guns. This had been going on for an hour now. His door was locked, and a man stood outside his window; and he still did not know what was happening.

Then he saw one of the dogs break free and go like a flash towards some bushes.

A small, dark-haired man ran desperately from the bushes, but in a moment he was surrounded by leaping dogs.

Roger saw what was nearly a miracle. The man flung one dog back, and it yelped and ran away. Another fell back, yapping, snarling. But there were too many of them.

It was impossible to watch any longer. Roger turned away, teeth clenched so hard that his jaws ached, nails biting into his palms. He did not know how long it was before he heard two shots, sounding a long way off because of the thick toughened glass of the window. He looked round again. The dark-haired man was being carried off, on a stretcher. The bodies of two dogs lay sprawled on the ground; and a man with a gun was turning away from them.

Carosi was there, now.

Then Julieta appeared.

Roger saw her running, hair streaming behind her, racing across the smooth grass towards the trees and the scene of the savage mauling. She looked as if she was berserk. Carosi tried to stop her, but she fended him off, then flung herself at the body of the first dog as a woman might fling herself at the body of a dead lover.

So Julieta was not empty of affection.

Carosi left her there for a few minutes, then gave an order, and two men pulled her off and led her away. She went submissively. But Roger saw the wildness in her eyes, and wondered if the paroxysm of grief had turned her mind. Then she was thrust out of his mind, for he saw the body of the man being carried towards a corner of the house. The light fell upon the dead man's face and lacerated throat, so that Roger could see clearly.

He recognised the dark-haired victim as one who had been jailed for a Carosi crime: a blackmailer named Dempster.

It looked as if Dempster had come to try to avenge himself.

But that wasn't all; that hardly mattered. If he knew Dempster as a Carosi man, so did everyone who mattered at the Yard. Gill, especially. If Dempster had been released from jail and come straight here, surely the Yard had arranged to follow him.

Roger looked towards the trees, as if he would see Gill and others coming through if he prayed hard enough.

The grounds emptied, and there was quiet again.

But his door was not unlocked, and he was kept in his room. He knew it was impossible to force it, he had tried too often; but he tried again, using a pick-lock fashioned out of a piece of wire from a lampshade which did not look damaged.

Poor raddled Maisie, with her gaudy make-up and lined face, her ducks and her dearies, brought him his meals, served as attractively as if this were a first-class hotel. She said very little today, and there was a scared look about her, as if the incident of the morning had frightened her.

Roger had no radio. The few books and magazines here bored him. He kept looking towards the trees, and knew that to set store by such hope was a sign of desperation. He had swallowed Carosi's bait, he had come just as he had planned, but now he was here he seemed helpless, could not even think and plan.

It was as if Carosi had sucked the vitality out of his mind.

This was a long, weary day.

The sky was beautiful in the evening, as darkness fell. Maisie came in with his dinner, drew the curtains, said: 'Oo, that woman's terrible today,' and went out. The door was locked behind her. Roger ate slowly, for the sake of something to do, then tried to read, but instead found his mind filled with wild ideas of escape, reaction against the sense of futility. By eleven o'clock, all the main lights were out, as far as he could tell. But for the guards the household was asleep. He went to the door, but gave up; he had no chance at all.

He needed one of those discs ...

But what good would it be to him if he had a hundred of them, and couldn't get away?

He went back to the window, caged and helpless, his nerves quivering and raw. Yet while he was here and alive there must *be* a chance; if he was alert every moment, one might come when he least expected it. If one came and he let it go, that would be the true failure.

He was awake and restless in the early hours when he heard a sound at the door. He was always locked in at night, but had never heard this before. He lay still, face turned to the door, eyes narrowed. He could see nothing, but there was a slight creaking sound, of the door opening. He expected to see a bright light beyond, but there was only a faint glow.

He saw a pale, ghostly figure.

He heard the door close, shutting out the light.

There was a rustling sound, but that was not all; he could smell a scent which Julieta used. Still he did not move, but he could imagine her face as she had flung herself at the dog, the hideous tension in it; and he remembered what Maisie had said about her.

She was very near.

'Roger,' she whispered, and he could only just hear the sound.
'Roger, wake up.'

No one here had ever called him Roger.

Why did she?

'Wake up,' Julieta repeated, and Roger felt her cold hand on his
shoulder, then her fingers gripping his arm tightly; her nails dug into
him. *'Wake up!'*

He started, as if suddenly awake.

'Who is it? What—' He jumped up, and thrust her hand away as
if in swift alarm. *'Who is it?'*

'Make no noise,' she whispered fiercely, and suddenly she thrust
herself against him, forcing him back, putting the weight of her
whole body on him. The softness of her breast smothered him;
unless he threw her off bodily he would choke.

She drew back ...

'If he finds me here he will kill me,' she said, and he was sure that
she believed that to be true. 'Be very quiet.'

He heard a different sound, the bedside light went on, and he saw
her.

She wore a flimsy, almost transparent white robe, lacy and billowy
and making her look quite beautiful. She had made up, as if for her
lover. She was smiling at him, too, and her lips were taut, as if she
was making herself smile.

Her eyes were burning.

'Look at me,' she ordered in that passionate whisper. 'Look at me!
Am I different from other women? Tell me that, now. Has he
destroyed me? Can I attract a man? *Can I?'*

She flung the robe back from her body.

She was the most beautiful thing he was ever likely to see: and
there was madness in her eyes.

He knew that the chance he had prayed for had come, that the
easiest thing would be to let it slip away. Give her reason to think
that she had been rebuffed, and she would turn into a raging term
agent. He must not take the risk, must soothe and delight her, must
do anything to make sure that she did not turn on him. For about

her neck hung a slim, golden chain, and attached to the chain, a red disc like the one he had seen before.

'Well, am I so different?' She thrust her head forward, he could see the quivering at her lips. 'Go on, tell me, am I so different from other women?'

Roger said in an unsteady voice: 'Different? You are as different from other women as gold is from brass.'

There was a moment of terrible silence.

He did not know what she would do, did not know whether he had said the thing she wanted. Then he saw fierce delight spread in her eyes. She flung herself forward, and hugged him fiercely. He held her tightly while she uttered wild, unintelligible things. He was reminded of Richard, his younger son, when very young and frightened, behaving like this, and pouring out all the causes of his fears.

He soothed and encouraged her.

'He is a devil, twists me, makes me indifferent to men; he won't let me live my own life—'

'It's all right, Julieta, you will live your own life soon.'

'I hate him, I hate him, I'll hate him for ever.'

'He won't worry you much longer, Julieta.'

'He made them kill my dogs, my beautiful dogs; he ordered them to be shot.'

'It's all right, Julieta, he won't do that again.'

'He's a devil, he makes men do his devilry; if they won't he kills them, or he takes away their wives. He always gets what he wants, he removes anyone who tries to stop him.'

'That will soon stop, Julieta.'

'Why don't you kill him?'

As she said that she drew back, seemed oblivious of her near nakedness. Then she thrust her face close to his, and spat the question out again.

'Why don't you kill him?'

Was this the moment of revelation? Was he to learn everything he needed to learn now? Did she know what Carosi was planning to do?

Roger said, gently: 'He mustn't be killed until we know what he is doing, Julieta. Then we can save a lot of people from great hurt.'

The fire faded from her eyes, she backed away a little, she looked puzzled as she asked: 'Why should I save others? Are they so important?'

'They will help you to become more normal, and—'

That was his undoing.

'Normal!' she cried, and leapt at him and struck him across the face time and time again, then drew back and hissed words at him, in a low-pitched voice which seemed to be the voice of evil itself. The madness flared up in her eyes.

'You say I am not normal, you dare insult me, insult *me,* Carosi's perfect woman. Wait until I tell him this! Wait until he knows the truth! I have tried to save you, I have persuaded him to let you live, but now I will tell him I found you in my room. I shall tell him you came into my room, and you tried to—'

Her voice was rising, and was nearly a screech; it would soon be heard outside. She stood there shaking clenched fists at him, her body quivering, the filmy, lacy robe shaking like a cascade of water; and the red disc danced and quivered against her lovely skin.

He had to silence her.

He snatched at her wrist and pulled her down, clasped his left hand over her mouth to stifle the scream, and gripped her throat tightly. He pressed his thumb against the windpipe. At first she kicked and struggled, but gradually the struggle ceased, and she went limp. He took his hands away, and waited, but she made no sound or movement. He pushed her away, towards the foot of the bed, got up, and then felt for her pulse; it was hard to be sure about it, for he himself was breathing so heavily.

She was alive; of course she was.

He twisted the little gold chain round so that he could get at the fastener, undid it, and slipped it, together with the disc, into the pocket of his jacket which hung on the back of a chair. Then he flung his clothes on. Julieta was stirring when he was dressed, but not awake. He tore a strip off the diaphanous gown, and wound it round and round her face, gagging her, and then went to the door. If she could open it, then surely he could.

He opened it.

There was a faint light from the hall.

He knew Julieta's room, and stepped towards it, making no sound on the thick carpet. He could see a man sitting near the great front door; a guard, to make doubly sure that there was no escape. He ignored this man and went back to Julieta's room, went in, and switched on the light. Her bed had been slept in; she must have tossed and turned before coming in to him. He went back for her, laid her on her own bed, and drew back.

She was still unconscious.

If he killed her, she would not be found until the morning, when he might be far away.

Should he kill her?

When she came round, would she be demented enough to tell Carosi what had happened? Or would her cunning make her fear the consequences of that too much? If she told part she must tell all, and Carosi would know that Roger could not have got out of his room and into hers.

She had lost that pass.

Roger felt her pulse again, and judged that she would be unconscious for some time yet; and for a long time after that would not know where she was, or what she was doing.

Should he kill?

Could he kill?

He turned away abruptly, and went out, closing her door very softly. Then he went down to the head of the stairs. The man was reading a book, and sitting so that he could see the foot of the stairs and the door; but until he looked up, he would see nothing.

Roger crept back to his room for a pillow, and then came back. For half the distance he could keep out of the guard's sight. He went down, step by step. The moment when he would be seen if the other glanced up, but the guard kept reading, as if enthralled. Roger went down, down, down, until he reached floor level. He moved to one side, now, so as to approach from behind.

He was out of sight when the man looked up, as if suspicious; and he was close enough to jump on the man and grip him round the throat, discarding the pillow as he went. He felt a convulsive heave of the man's body, but he choked the wild cry, and gripped with all his strength.

He heard a sharp crack of sound, and knew that he had broken this man's neck.

He let him go, then took the gun from his pocket and put it in his own. He made sure that the red disc was safe, then stepped to the door, and began to unfasten the chains, the bolts and the locks. One of them would have the electric switch built in; every moment was one of screaming tension, in case an alarm bell clanged.

It did not.

He opened the door and stepped into the grounds.

Chapter Sixteen

The Irishman

It was not often that Detective-Sergeant Gill saw the Assistant Commissioner alone, and Gill stood somewhat in awe of Chatworth. Yet during the past few days, normality had gone by the board at Scotland Yard, and after reading a report with more than usual interest, Gill got up from his desk and was soon at Chatworth's door, giving a tap which sounded peremptory because he was so nervous.

Chatworth looked surprised at the sight of him, but was affable enough.

'Good morning, sergeant. What can I do for you?'

'If you can spare me five minutes, sir.'

'Yes. What's it all about?'

Greatly encouraged, Gill approached the desk.

'I've just read that an old lag named Dempster came out of prison a fortnight ago, sir. Inside for putting on the black. Suspected of working for Carosi, too. He was a footman at Sir Mortimer Grant's house for a while. Do you remember him, sir?'

'Vaguely,' said Chatworth. 'What's he been doing?'

'He's the only man who ever had any dealings with Carosi whom we've been able to trace lately. I arranged for a special watch—there's a chance that he'll try to contact Carosi pretty soon. And he's gone to Ireland—arrived there late last night on the last 'plane from Croydon. Batten, the man following him, managed to get on the same 'plane. Dempster hired a car in Dublin, and drove through the night to Killarney. Batten's just telephoned from there, sir. He couldn't follow by road, but managed to get a morning 'plane to the Shannon airport, and then went on by road. He had a word with the Civic Guards, who knew Dempster was in Killarney early this morning but don't know where he went.'

'Dempster got any relatives or association with Killarney?' Chatworth demanded.

'None that I can trace, sir,' said Gill.

'Hm,' said Chatworth. 'Very long shot to think he might have gone to Carosi, but you're even more desperate to find him than I am. Bad thing about West. His wife—' Chatworth broke off. 'Well, we mustn't miss a chance. Think Batten is lonely at Killarney by himself?'

'I don't think he ought to be left on his own,' said Gill, 'and I thought you would like to ask the co-operation of the Civic Guards—they're very touchy over there.'

'So would I be if they came here!' said Chatworth. 'I'll speak to Dublin police right away. It's a bit thin, but we don't want Batten being chivvied across Eire.'

'No, sir. There's one other thing. Dempster was released on the same day as Willie the Squealer, who—'

'Even I know Willie the Squealer,' said Chatworth.

'He and Dempster were in the same squad at Parkmoor,' Gill explained. 'You know how it is in stir, sir—they talk much more freely than they do outside. Dempster might have talked to Willie. So I thought if I tackled Willie—'

'Let me know what he says,' said Chatworth. 'And what about Mrs West, Gill?' He was very gruff. 'Would it help if I went to see her again?'

'She'd appreciate it, sir, and she's taking it on the chin. Nothing will persuade her that Handsome—that Mr West is dead, sir.'

Divisional DO's picked up Willie the Squealer in his single-room 'apartment' in a dark hovel near the Hundred Arches. Willie protested whiningly when he was taken to the Wapping Police

Station. He was going straight. Why, he hadn't lifted a finger since he'd come out.

He looked surprised to see the massive Gill, who stood in the charge-room at the Wapping Station, a very different man from the nervous sergeant at Scotland Yard.

The other detectives went out.

'Now what's this?' demanded Willie edgily. 'I haven't done nothing and I ain't got anything to say, you needn't think I have.'

'We're not trying to pin anything on you, Willie, take it easy,' said Gill. 'Anything you say is for my ears alone—that's why I sent the others out. I'm at the Yard now.'

'You never deserved promotion,' muttered Willie.

'You don't deserve this,' said Gill, offering cigarettes, 'and you ought still to be inside, but here you are, free as the air. Meet any nice boys in jug?'

Willie lit the cigarette.

'There ain't none,' he declared.

'Not even you, Willie? Some are worse than others, though. Hear anything about Carosi?'

Willie's face twitched.

'Oo?'

'Carosi. Chap who was causing some trouble before you went in,' said Gill casually.

'Never 'eard of him!'

'Haven't you?' asked Gill, softly. 'Dempster had his knife into Carosi, didn't he?'

'What?' screeched Willie. He jumped up, dropping the cigarette, tried to save it from falling, and burnt himself. 'Dempster always said—now, listen,' he added, bending down to retrieve the cigarette, and refusing to meet Gill's eyes. 'I don't know nothing about Carosi. Forget it.'

'Willie, you're a poor liar,' Gill said. 'You were working at the same bench as Dempster. Carosi shopped him, and Dempster went to get his own back.'

'It's no use,' declared Willie stubbornly. 'I dunno a thing.'

'Willie,' murmured Gill, 'there was a little bit of bag-snatching in Mile End Road three days ago. You were seen near the incident. And you've just come out, so you're stranded. I don't say j'ou did the job. That's up to the court. But you'd have a job to prove you—'

'You ruddy, lying copper!' snarled Willie. 'I wasn't anywhere near, wouldn't touch anyfink with a bargepole; you can't pin it on me!'

'What did Dempster say?' asked Gill.

Willie drew a deep breath, and then capitulated.

'S'matter o' fact, 'e did 'ave it in for Carosi,' he muttered. 'Said 'e knew where to find 'im, an' as soon as 'e could get enough ready together, 'e'd be arter 'im. But I told 'im 'e was a fool, 'e'd never get nowhere with Carosi.'

'And you'd never heard of Carosi, hadn't you?' asked Gilt, with heavy sarcasm. 'All right, Willie, scram.'

Gill was met at Rynnenna airport next day by a huge, red-faced Captain of the Civic Guard, who rejoiced in the name of Mulloon, a tremendous thirst, and a professed admiration for any and everything English, including the representatives of Scotland Yard. And he had a car – what a car! It was a huge glistening Chrysler, and roared along the poor road from Rynnenna to the south.

Mulloon told story after story of the villainies of the English. Whenever he spotted a ruin, he would stop the car and invite Gill to gaze upon it, and remark that it was the finest ruin in the whole of Kerry, and if it hadn't been for the man Cromwell, now, it would still be a fine castle.

''Twould and all,' said Mulloon. 'The damage that man did, ye'd never believe.'

'I didn't know him,' remarked Gill, blandly.

'Och, it's no use pretending ye wouldn't do the same today if ye had the chance,' said Mulloon, 'but don't mistake me, Sergeant, I like the English—och, yes, I like the English, they're the finest creatures on God's earth if ye forget the Irish. And the Americans. And maybe one or two others of the lesser races—come, man!' He slapped Gill across the shoulders and started the car off again. 'It's only jokin' that I am. A fine time I've had with your man Batten.'

They tore into Killarney.

It was market day, and the three main streets were still crowded with people and cattle. Soon they drew up outside the Great Southern Hotel, near the railway station. Mulloon jumped out as soon as the car stopped, and rested a hand on Gill's arm.

"'Tis a fine hotel ye're coming to, Sergeant, the finest in all Ireland!'

He led the way across a large hall and then to a gloomy staircase; next across a large hall into a large double room with twin beds, where big and burly Detective-Officer Batten was poring over a map spread out on a small table.

Batten jumped up.

'Anything Dick?' asked Gill.

'Not much,' said Batten. 'I've marked a dozen big, private houses, but they all seem to belong to Americans!'

'That needn't worry us,' said Gill. 'Carosi would probably call himself an American. Any with dogs?'

'Now, what would a man in a big house be doing if he hadn't some dogs to keep him company. If it's a greyhound ye want, I've a friend who has the fastest—'

'Alsatians,' said Batten.

'I wouldn't be trusting the brutes,' said Mulloon.

'Does anyone near by have a private aeroplane?' asked Gill.

'Well, now, if there aren't three or four,' said Mulloon. "'Tis a fine country for flying, they tell me, and only a step across the water to America itself. Alsatian dogs, now. And aeroplanes. And what else would ye be looking for? This Carosi man. If so, it's the wrong place ye've come to, Sergeant; we wouldn't have a wicked criminal like Carosi in a fine part of Ireland like this. Would we, now?'

'Well, I don't know,' said Gill. 'You had Cromwell.'

Mulloon's big eyes rounded, his full lips parted with a hiss. There was a moment of utter stillness before he roared with laughter, slapped Gill boisterously on the back, and went off into another paroxysm.

When Mulloon recovered, he said weakly: 'Sure and that's the finest crack I've heard from an Englishman in all me nach'ral,

Sergeant. It's a smart man ye are, and ye'll get everything from Pat Mulloon that he can give ye. Och, we had Cromwell!' He went off into another paroxysm of laughter, while Batten watched him exasperatedly. 'Now where are we?' he demanded at last. "Tis a man named Carosi with an aeroplane and Alsatian dogs ye're looking for, and it's the glamorous Inspector West who is alive if he isn't dead.'

'That's right,' said Gill, quietly.

'Och, we can't have men going about Ireland, with a famous English detective as a prisoner, it wouldn't do at all. Pat Mulloon looks a bit of a fool, no doubt, but he knows what goes on in Killarney. It's an idea I'm having. Ye wouldn't be liking Michael O'Leary.'

Batten stirred restlessly.

'No, that man Michael O'Leary had a great-great-grandfather whose great-great-grandfather owned a castle which became a Cromwell ruin, that's the truth as I'm standing here,' Mulloon declared. 'And Michael O'Leary is the fine upstanding officer in charge at Kerry. A great one for talking, is Michael O'Leary, for all he's a man with a remarkable keen sense of observation, and only a week ago he was talking to me. "Pat," he said to me, "ye've heard me talk of the American millionaire who bought Kinara?" "Yes, Michael," I said, and I didn't remind him I'd seldom heard him talk of anything else; this American was a great man who bought Kinara five years ago, or would it be six? I'm trying to think of his name, now.' Mulloon struck an attitude of deep concentration. 'Och, that is it, Pyne!—Jacon C. Pyne, as ever was, and so rich you would never believe. He bought Kinara, the house and the grounds and the wood, and all, did ye ever see such woods? In a circle they are, surrounding the grounds of the house; och, they must stretch for miles. And the old Earl of Kinara had a great high wall built around it, and oak trees planted both sides of the wall; 'tis a lonely spot and haunted by the Devil himself, if ever there was such a place in all of Ireland. And Michael O'Leary was telling me that this Pyne has a private aeroplane, och, yes I And the grounds stretch down to the coast into the bargain. All manner of boats he had, from yawls to yachts and steam-launches and—were ye saying something, Sergeant Gill?'

'No, no,' said Gill, hastily. 'You go on, Captain.'

'There isn't much more to tell ye,' declared Mulloon. 'Michael O'Leary never wearies of telling me how often the man Pyne goes up in his aeroplane; why, 'tis even suggested he has a pair of them. And 'tis said that the shopkeepers never go inside the grounds, they deliver everything at the lodge, and I *have* heard talk of big dogs.'

'Dogs!' cried Batten, unable to restrain himself. 'Now, don't get excited,' cautioned Mulloon, ''tis well known that the Irish often exaggerate. But there's another small thing, maybe it will help ye. By the strangest coincidence I spoke to O'Leary on the telephone early this morning. "Mike," said I, "I've a fine, powerful Englishman from Scotland Yard taking the air at Killarney, who says he came after a man named Dempster who left Killarney early yesterday morning; a little dark-haired fellow, this Dempster. Did ye see the like of him near Kinara?" I asked, and would ye believe it, Mike O'Leary said to me: "There was talk of a dark-haired man who didn't look like an Englishman and went towards Kinara yesterday morning, and climbed the great wall—and after that he wasn't seen again."'

Batten exclaimed: 'We've got him!'

'Now don't get excited, me boys,' cautioned Mulloon again. ''Tis an English habit to get excited when there's no reason and to go to sleep when they've every cause to wake up. This Pyne isn't your Carosi. According to the description in the newspapers, Carosi is a short, square kind of man, and Pyne is tall and thin. If ye take my advice, ye'll consult O'Leary and make arrangements with him to visit Kinara, and if ye take my advice again,' added Mulloon solemnly, 'I'd telephone Scotland Yard and have Scotland Yard telephone Dublin and have Dublin telephone O'Leary, to tell him what to do, or he won't do it. And if this Mr Pyne is giving sanctuary to your Carosi, it would take a small army to raid Kinara. I'd be very careful if I was you.'

A hundred eyes seemed to be watching Roger that night, but he reached the pitch-darkness of the nearest oak tree without an alarm being raised. He looked back. All he could see was the dark outline of the great pile – there was no crack of light anywhere.

He listened tensely for the sound of patrolling men, and the night seemed filled with the lurking shapes of wild dogs. They were loose by night, he knew, and were his greatest danger. And in this darkness he could go round and round. He must wait at least until dawn.

Unless ...

A dog began to bark, not far away.

At him?

He walked on, every step an ordeal. The howling and barking stopped, but it seemed to Roger that above the sound of his own footsteps there was the padding of the paws of twenty straining beasts. The fringe of trees, with the moon behind, gave a deep shadow.

The dogs began again, and now he knew that it was not at him. Hope surged. He still went on, telling himself that the wall of the grounds could not be far away.

Then dogs began to howl behind him. He glanced round and saw the wolf-like shapes heading towards him in a pack, with two or three strung out in the lead.

Then he heard a sharp crack of sound, and a flash lit up the darkness ahead.

Roger saw a high wall, and a man sitting astride it, bright in another flash. Then a powerful light lit the whole of the grounds near here, dazzling Roger, dazzling the dogs. He blundered on, then heard a voice he had almost lost hope of ever hearing again: 'This way, Roger!' bellowed Gill. 'This way.'

'Now this is going to be a fight, me boyo,' said Mulloon to O'Leary.

Mulloon and O'Leary were still astride the wall. Gill and several others had jumped down. A group of Carosi's men was fleeing across the parkland, with as many Civic Guards in full cry after them, but the shooting was spasmodic.

Roger stood near the wall.

He had hardly grown used to the fact that Gill and Batten, with a strong company of Civic Guards, had been waiting to raid it when the dogs had started howling and the shooting had begun. And now the fighting near the wall was all but over. At least a dozen of Carosi's men were dead or captured. Most of the dogs were dead; no live ones were in sight. Little groups of men were standing about and talking. There were still no lights in the house.

Gill's hand rested on Roger's arm.

'Feeling all right, Roger?'

'I'm fine,' said Roger. 'Gill, I'll never be able—'

'Well, now, if it isn't the great Inspector West!' boomed Mulloon, bustling forward from a group of men. 'It's a proud man I am to know ye, Inspector!' He thrust out a great hand. 'And it's glad ye are to see me, ye needn't be telling me, a fine hearty night it's been. Meet me friend, Captain O'Leary of County Kerry; it's O'Leary ye have to thank.'

'Will ye keep your great voice quiet a minute, we cannot hear ourselves speak,' said O'Leary. He shook hands vigorously. ''Tis a pleasure to meet Inspector West,' he declared, 'and a good night's work, ye'll be agreeing. Will ye come and help us raid the house itself?'

'It can't be soon enough,' Roger said, 'we should find all of Carosi's records and—'

A sheet of flame lit up the grey night, and the great house was suddenly a blaze of light. There came the roaring boom of an explosion, then a blast which carried them off their feet.

As they recovered, a dull, red glow showed through a glassless window of the house.

As they ran, Roger realised that there was no hope of saving Kinara.

He heard aeroplanes taking off, and knew that Carosi had escaped.

And how he would hate, now.

Chapter Seventeen

Carosi Proposes

Julieta sat in a deck-chair on board the motor cruiser. On the bridge, the little Captain, Marco, looked down at the bows where Carosi stood, his hands clasped behind him like a pocket Hitler, surveying the empty waste of water. There was no other ship in sight; no land.

Carosi had been standing there for nearly two hours since they had vanished in the early morning mist. Julieta had been conscious when men had come in, to waken her and to carry her to safety.

Julieta could not see him.

A white-jacketed steward came round the cabin and approached her. His impassive face gave no indication of the crisis through which they were passing, although every member of the crew knew what had happened in Kinara.

'Mr Carosi would like to see you, Miss.'

'Very well,' said Julieta, but instead of going straight to Carosi, she leaned against the rail. She had on no lipstick or rouge and her face was pallid and drawn. Only her eyes were bright, and they held a strange, wild glow. She lit a cigarette, tossed the match into the sea, then went towards Carosi.

'You have been a long time.' His hoarse voice had not changed. 'What is the matter with you? Are you ill?'

'No,' said Julieta. 'I'm not ill. I am just—eaten up with hatred.'

'For West?'

She said: 'For everyone who helped to do it.' Her lips hardly moved. 'And you were so sure they could not find out. Even you have failed.'

'I *never* fail,' said Carosi.

'You have failed. Even you. So much boasting, so much confidence, and now—failure. Everything gone. Everything.'

'You are hysterical,' said Carosi, flatly. 'You do not shout or scream, but it is the same thing. I am tired of your behaviour. You have been like this since two dogs died on the day that Dempster came. He injured them, so they had to be killed. So you should not waste affection on animals of any kind.'

She looked at him with that curious intensity.

'Men—women—dogs—they are all animals to you. Just animals. You use them, but you have no affection for them, they do not matter. What *are* you?'

'I am a rational man,' said Carosi. 'And you have been a rational woman until now. We are not in such a serious position as you imagine. I have not failed – I, Carosi, to fail?' A new and menacing note sounded in his voice, which grew deep and unfamiliar. 'I will not have you talk such nonsense! With all my plans, my great conception all ready to put into action—am I to be stopped by such a thing as this? You are losing your faith when I need your loyalty most. Remember all I have done for you. Your life of luxury. Your servants. Everything you owe to me.'

She didn't answer.

'You see, Julieta,' went on Carosi, 'I am going on with my plans. And they will succeed. The loss of Kinara' – he shrugged – 'it was not welcome, it was not expected, but I had prepared against it. It was unfortunate that Dempster, one man who knew where to find the house, had been released from prison, but—'

'Talk!' she spat at him. 'You are just a windbag of words!'

Carosi took his hands from behind his back and struck her across the face. The blow sent her staggering to one side. Her eyes blazed, she looked as if she could fly at him, but regained her balance and stood still.

'It was a set-back, no more. In all, twenty-seven men were lost. Including Pyne. I am sorry about Pyne, because he was so valuable in America. But there are still more than a hundred men and some twenty women waiting to receive orders. They will receive them. West escaped, but does not know what I plan. All the documents at Kinara were destroyed. You see how carefully I had prepared for any emergency.'

'You had a hundred men and twenty women waiting to receive instructions,' said Julieta fiercely. 'Will they be now? Every newspaper is full of the disaster. Everyone is laughing at you. All your own people will read the newspapers. How can they trust a man who allows such a disaster to happen?'

'Julieta,' began Carosi softly, '*I* will not permit—'

'Listen to me!' she screeched at him. 'Forget that you are always so right, listen to *me*. We know the people, the fools. Hardly any of them are like Pyne and Maisie, who would always remain loyal. Most of them are mean, cruel and easily frightened. Scared to death in case they offended you, compelled to obey while you were all-powerful, but now – *scared of the police as well*. You taught them to believe that the police could not harm them if they had your protection. Now all that is over.'

'Every little fool will be scurrying around, trying to make sure *he* doesn't get hurt. Nine out of ten will fail you because they've never learned to act or think for themselves. They all depend on you.'

'But I am here, I shall instruct them,' said Carosi. His voice was a grating sound in his throat.

'But they cannot be sure of you any more!' cried Julieta. 'I will tell you what you should do. Go away! Leave Europe! Give up your plans. Only a fool would think he could succeed now.'

'You have lost faith,' said Carosi heavily. He squared his shoulders. 'I am sorry for you. Two dogs die—and you become a hysterical fool. Now I am beginning to ask myself questions. *Has* this change come about *just* because of two dogs?'

Julieta said: 'I loved them.'

'I made a mistake when I allowed you to give your affection to those animals; I should not have allowed you to have affection for any living thing,' Carosi said. 'You have disappointed me, Julieta. But I do not believe that you behave like this because of the dogs. It is something else. I have never known you behave over a man as you have over West. You pleaded for him from the first. You were anxious that he should not be tortured. Anxious that I should talk to him freely. You did not want him hurt. A very good-looking man, yes. An Adonis. The first man to make your heart beat fast. The first man—'

'No!' cried Julieta. 'It is not true!'

Carosi shot out his hand and caught her wrist. He drew her nearer, and looked down coldly, unfeelingly.

'Tell me the truth,' he said, twisting. 'Admit it'

The sun shone on to her eyes, and she tried hard to keep them open.

'Julieta, tell me the truth,' said Carosi, and his voice seemed to grind itself into her ears.

She cried. 'Yes, yes, yes, it's true! You tried to make me inhuman, tried to crush every spark of natural affection out of me, tried to make me a machine, a machine with a cruel mind and a perfect body. You made me indifferent to men, and yet men gazed at me with terrible passion. You robbed me of my birthright. You made sure that I should never know the thrill and wonder of real passion, and then *he* came. And I compared him with you. I saw a man who could be hard and terrible, yet so soft and kind. And I wanted to see how you behaved when you were together. I came and heard you talk to him, and I matched you against each other. West is a *man*. You—'

Carosi's left hand moved to her throat. She flinched but made no effort to get away. His pressure grew tighter, and she made a choking noise.

Julieta's face became tinged with red, her breasts heaved as she struggled silently for breath. Her eyes began to close. Then Carosi released her, and flung her aside.

She was alone in her cabin. The marks of Carosi's fingers and thumbs were on her wrist and throat. She sat staring out of the port-hole, as the ship moved quietly and steadily on.

She had been here for an hour.

She heard a man approaching along a corridor, but did not look up when the door opened.

It was Carosi.

He stepped in briskly, closed the door behind him, went to a small cupboard and got out a bottle of whisky. He took glasses from the little railed shelf, and poured out two drinks. He gave her one, and she took it without looking at him.

'We shall berth a little after dark,' said Carosi, 'and we have a great deal to do before then. Instructions to our agents must be sent out tonight. You will prepare the messages and the codes.'

Julieta sipped her drink.

'The first step will be to take Mortimer Grant and his friends away, before we take the others,' went on Carosi. 'If they cannot be taken away, they will have to be killed.'

Julieta sneered: 'You promised West you would not harm them. You always keep your promises.'

'The situation is different now,' said Carosi. 'Let us have no more argument.'

He left her.

Chapter Eighteen

Counter Measures

Roger saw the light on at his Bell Street house as he was driven up to it. The sergeant driver jumped out to open his door, then said: 'Good night, sir.' Roger hardly heard him, his heart was pounding so much.

The door opened, and there was Janet.

There was life.

'I'd feel on top of the world if Chatworth would tell you that you must go away and leave Carosi to the others,' said Janet, as they lay together in bed, close, warm, content. 'But I suppose I might as well wish for the moon.'

'I don't think you really want me to give Carosi to someone else, now that he's on the run.'

'Don't be too confident, darling,' cautioned Janet, slowly. 'He won't be easy.'

'He's going to be as tough as they ever come,' agreed Roger, 'but although he'll lose hard, he'll lose.'

He thought a lot about Carosi, and as much about Julieta, and he wondered if he would ever tell Janet about Carosi's ward. He was awake long after Janet went to sleep.

It was surprising how quickly things were back to normal. Breakfast, the boys boisterous with delight at seeing him again, welcome home from several neighbours, Janet's kiss a little more passionate perhaps ...

Then the Yard; a hundred hands to shake, a hundred voices wishing him well, the newspapers splashing his name and photograph.

Chatworth was alone in his office. A chair was pulled up for Roger, and Chatworth pushed the silver cigarette-box across.

'Now, Roger—the lot, please.'

'Before I go back to the motor-boat trick, I ought to confirm what I arranged by telephone yesterday,' said Roger. 'Sir Mortimer Grant, Dana, Raffety and Harrison are being watched from a distance, because I think Carosi will have a cut at them. The prisoners taken at Kinara are all in England now, and are being questioned. I telephoned New York and asked the Police Department for a report on Pyne. He was caught trying to get out after the fire,' went on Roger. 'He hasn't said much yet, but I think he'll crack. He's over at Cannon Row, sir. The woman Maisie is in our nursing-home. Fingleton's back on duty, but I doubt if he'll touch this job now.'

'And that leaves Michael Grant,' Chatworth said.

'I still don't know what to make of him,' said Roger. 'If the woman Julieta was right, he was allowed to take his Christine away because he'd helped Carosi. I've talked to Superintendent Morris, who questioned Grant closely, without learning anything. He's being watched at a distance, too. I don't think any of the people we're watching will get away. We've arranged for a walkie-talkie radio to be used wherever possible, and the hunt for Carosi's men as well as Carosi couldn't be fiercer, sir. And we're checking the red disc, or pass—it seems to be a kind of identification tag. Anyone who has one will be held at once.'

'Good. Now let me have your own story,' Chatworth said.

That took a long time.

As Roger talked, he felt the queer, almost hypnotic influence of Carosi; even here in this room it was as if the man was watching him, mocking him. This was reflected in his voice, and affected Chatworth, too. When it was told, Chatworth said very slowly: 'We haven't any idea what he's up to, have we?'

'None, sir.'

'The little red disc is the best we have for a clue.'

'Yes.'

'And you're still scared, in case Carosi pulls it off,' said Chatworth.

'Yes,' admitted Roger slowly, and said what he had kept from Janet. 'I'm scared because I think that after this he'll be so vicious that he'll be more cold-blooded than ever. He'll do all the harm he can for the sake of it, and—'

'I'd ordered a guard back and front at your home,' Chatworth said. 'I'll have it doubled.'

'Thank you, sir,' Roger said, and went on: 'I'm going to see the Grants, sir. I can't understand why Carosi let them go, it's been bothering me all the time. It wasn't simply reward for services rendered. Carosi must have had some purpose or a good reason.'

'See what you can do,' Chatworth said, and Roger realised that he looked very tired. 'Carosi's scared me, too,' the AC admitted. 'I feel as if I'm sitting on top of a volcano which is going to erupt any minute.'

'I know just what you mean,' Roger said.

He went out, and hurried along the passage towards the front hall, passing his own office as the door opened. He didn't want any of the CI's who shared the office to delay him, but he did not go fast enough, for Eddie Day called out: 'Handsome!'

'Can't stop,' Roger called.

'You must!' insisted Eddie, and came lumbering along the passage. 'Everything's gone haywire in this last half-hour,' he grumbled. 'Trouble all over the place. Smash-and-grabs -hold ups—every ruddy crook in the country seems to be busy this morning. Think it's Carosi's big show?'

Roger felt as if that volcano was beginning to erupt.

A car engine roared outside and drove out of the Yard. Another engine started up, and someone shouted along another passage: 'We want every Flying Squad man on duty. Rout 'em all out!'

'See what I mean,' said Eddie. 'All the Divisions are asking for Squad cars—and there's a riot down Mile End Road. Brewster's gang and Red Finnigan's mob are mixing it. *I* think it's Carosi!'

'It may be,' said Roger.

If it was, what chance was there of stopping the man?

Gill turned into the passage and came hurrying towards them, his face bright with excitement.

'You've heard, sir?'

'I've been telling him,' said Eddie, complainingly, 'and I don't think he believes me.'

'Looks like *it*,' said Gill, trying to keep his voice low. 'Biggest thing since I've been at the Yard. It doesn't matter where you look, there's trouble. Been two big hold-ups in Oxford Street, one in Piccadilly.'

'What are we going to do?' shrilled Eddie.

Roger said: 'I'm going to see the Grants. Stay here, Gill. Don't go out unless you're forced to, and summarize all the reports.'

Gill said eagerly, as Eddie moved off:

'I think this is it, Roger. It's like an eruption. Everything's happening at once, exactly the kind of wholesale scoop that Carosi would try to pull off.'

'Could be,' said Roger. He hated even to think it, but at heart he knew that it was true. 'I won't be any longer than I can help.'

He hurried on, hearing two more Flying Squad cars snorting off.

'Bit of a do, sir, isn't it?' asked a sergeant. 'This is it all right.'

'Looks like it,' said Roger. 'Telephone my house, will you, and ask Mrs West to stay indoors today until she hears from me.'

'I'll see to it, sir.'

'Thanks,' said Roger, and hurried on his way.

Did Grant know anything, he wondered? Could he be made to talk?

Why had Carosi let him and Christine go?

Gill had the most exciting hours of his life. He sat in the Information Room, with another sergeant, an inspector and two detective-officers, and watched little multi-coloured pins being stuck into huge maps of London and its environs which hung all round the walls. He noted reports as they came through with increasing momentum. A big store was raided by half-a-dozen armed men, furs and jewellery were loaded into private cars and driven off. Almost simultaneously, three smaller fur shops in Oxford Street were raided.

In the West End, the City and the suburbs, it was crime with the lid off. Every Flying Squad car had already been detailed to a certain area, the Divisional HQs were ringing up one after the other for more help. The gang-fight in the Mile End Road was the forerunner of several in the East End. At the Elephant and Castle, Aldgate, Bethnal Green and Limehouse, the rioting drove the people off the streets and held up traffic until, along some main roads, there were lines of cars nearly a mile long.

By half past eleven, the first report of a hold-up at a City bank was soon followed by three others. Two safe deposits were entered. Armed and masked men held up cashiers and shop-keepers, took what ready money there was available, and made off.

Only a few were caught, and each of these carried one of the little red discs, obviously both pass and identification tag.

By midday, after a hurried consultation with the Home Office, Chatworth asked for military assistance to keep the streets clear and to reinforce the Flying Squad.

Soon trouble started in the provinces. The police of Manchester, Birmingham, Cardiff, Bristol, Sheffield, Liverpool, Newcastle, Edinburgh, Glasgow and Hull were all on the telephone to Scotland Yard, reporting a condition not far removed from chaos – and reporting the considered opinion of the local CIDs that this was Carosi's big day. Special watch was kept on ports and airports to make sure that the goods stolen, which amounted to over a million pounds by midday, weren't taken out of the country. Arrests were being made in all these centres and in London, and still everyone had the red discs. In spite of the arrests, there was no slackening in the outbreak.

No one at the Yard doubted that the eruption had been carefully organized, that the simultaneous outrages had been calculated to strain the resources of the police to breaking-point. Gradually a pattern could be discerned in the chaos -a pattern made by a cold, logical and ruthless mind.

How far would it go?

So far, none of the men known to have been blackmailed by Carosi had been visited, all seemed normal.

Everything was normal at Grant's London apartment until Roger West arrived. When the door was opened Michael Grant and his wife stood together, with little Arthur Morely near them in meek silence.

Chapter Nineteen

Family Party

'Well, well,' Roger said as the door closed behind him, and it was hard to keep the sneer out of his voice. 'Quite a family party. What are you celebrating?'

Morely just looked at him reproachfully.

Christine said: 'Please, Mr West,' and stopped.

Grant said: 'You'd better come in,' and led the way into a fine room, with modern furniture, and great windows, overlooking one of London's lovelier squares. When they were all there, he went on: 'You think I'm a heel. Right. I let Carosi go once, and helped him a second time, because I considered my first duty was to my wife. I'd do it all again. If you think I enjoyed doing it, you're wrong.'

His wife looked so very lovely, yet not radiant now: acutely distressed.

'And I think my son-in-law was right,' Morely put in, gently. 'What do you think you would have done in the same circumstances, Mr West?'

'I don't know,' Roger said harshly. 'I didn't have to try myself out. I haven't come here to pass judgement on whether you did the right or the wrong thing, Grant. I came to find out if you know anything you haven't yet told us.'

'I do not.'

Roger flashed a red disc in front of his eyes.

'Have you ever seen one of these before?'

He looked into Grant's face, and saw how pale it was, felt quite sure that Grant had seen such a disc. Did the sight of it frighten him?

'No,' he said brusquely.

'Don't lie, Grant. If you—'

Grant raised his head and spoke in clipped, angry tones: 'Don't shout at me, and don't call me a liar. My answer was no. That's final.'

'Listen to me,' Roger said icily. 'Outside, thousands of people are being robbed, many being injured, some being killed. That is Carosi's work. There is just a chance we might be able to stop it before it becomes too late. There's something else: Carosi has your father and several other wealthy people under his thumb. Nothing has happened to them yet, but it's likely to before long. If only for your father's sake—'

'I've never seen one of those discs before.'

'*All* right,' said Roger, savagely, 'you've never seen one before. I still think you're a liar. Now—'

He saw Christine Grant move forward. Grant had seemed to be avoiding her deliberately, but Roger paused to let her speak, and Grant could not avoid her when she said: 'Michael, it's time you told the whole truth.' When he didn't answer, she took his arm and Roger could almost feel the pressure of her grip, could hear anguish in her voice. 'I know why you've helped Carosi, I know that you're afraid of what he might do to me if he ever finds out that you've tried to help the police. But I can't live on other people's lives any longer. If Carosi isn't caught, whenever he robs and blackmails and kills I shall think that I owe my life to it—to every crime he's ever committed.'

'Don't talk like that!' Grant cried.

'But it's the truth, Mike, it's the simple truth. Do you think I could ever be really happy? Could you?'

Grant looked tormented.

Morely murmured, more softly even than usual: 'I'm sure the Inspector would not inform anyone who had told him—'

Grant snatched at the disc in Roger's hand.

'All right,' he rasped, 'I've seen one of these. My father had one. I've seen other men show him one when they went to see him. That was when I first discovered there was trouble. But that's all I know. How far does that help you?'

'Have you seen anybody else carrying them?'

'No.' Grant's arm was held about Christine's waist as he went on: 'There isn't another thing I know to help, West; you're only wasting your time.'

There was just one more question to ask: 'Why did Carosi let you go?'

'I've told you often enough. I struck a bargain with him, my wife's safety for his. He kept his side of it. I hope to God I don't live to regret not keeping mine.'

Roger went out to his car, feeling cold and helpless. He flicked on the radio, and heard the flurried comments from the Information Room. The situation was even more chaotic than it had been, there seemed to be no end to it. He asked if there was any special news of Sir Mortimer Grant, Raffety, Dana and Harrison, and there was none. He drove back to the Yard, with the feeling that the key that he was looking for lay within his grasp, and that it had to do with Carosi's reasons for freeing Michael Grant and Christine.

Sentiment? The keeping of a bargain? He didn't believe that either was possible. It must have been to Carosi's advantage or he must have done it under pressure.

Under pressure?

Could anyone exert such pressure that Carosi would give way?

Why had he released the Grants?

Roger caught his breath as a new idea flashed into his mind. He pulled into the side of the road and let himself think over it, and the more he thought, the more possible it seemed. He flicked his radio on, and *Information Room* answered quickly.

'West here. Put me through to the Assistant Commissioner at once.'

'Yes, sir.'

Hurry, hurry, hurry!

'That you, West?' Chatworth sounded gruff and tired, and made it clear that he did not expect good news.

Roger said, tensely: 'I've just seen a new angle, sir, and it might take us just where we want to go. I've thought of a possible reason for Carosi allowing the Grants to leave Kinara. Supposing one of Carosi's associates, one of great importance, didn't want them hurt? A relation, who—'

'Are you crazy?' Chatworth interrupted. 'Sir Mortimer Grant has been a victim of Carosi for ten years or more!'

'I wasn't thinking of Sir Mortimer Grant,' said Roger. 'I'm thinking of a man who came out of prison just before all this began. Until he was released, Carosi was out of the country. Soon after, Carosi came back to start afresh. The man I mean has been in and out of it all the time, just a pathetic old man who seemed to be hovering near the fringe of it, but—'

'Do you mean Arthur Merely?' Chatworth almost screamed.

'I mean Arthur Morely,' said Roger. 'Don't shout me down, sir, but listen. It did begin after Morely came out of prison. He's kept cropping up in this, too. He's obviously deeply fond of his daughter. Carosi as we know him wouldn't have hesitated to kill Grant, but something made him stop. Both Grant and his wife could have been killed: they weren't. If Morely's involved, he could have forced Carosi to hold his hand. I think we ought to have Morely trailed everywhere he goes, but it's got to be done so well that he won't know that he's being followed.'

There was a pause before Chatworth said: 'Well, at least it can't do any harm.'

The police kept track of Arthur Morely everywhere he went. Unexpectedly, he went towards the London docks after leaving his daughter and son-in-law, to tea at a dockers' cafe, and watched ships and barges unloading. Now and again he stared across the river, where barges were loading large barrels. Sometimes he smiled. Then he began to inquire for work aboard ship. Several times he was refused brusquely, but eventually he was told that the *Snow Queen,* at Simley's Wharf down river, was hard up for men for a six months' voyage.

He got a job, and spent the night at a hostel near Simley's Wharf. All this, Roger knew.

But he almost forgot it in the news sensation – the disappearance of wealthy men and men in high positions. Not only Raffety, Sir Mortimer Grant, Dana and Harrison were affected, but men in social, business and political spheres were disappearing by the dozen.

From early morning till late evening, men of great renown and repute had left their homes, their offices or their clubs, and had not returned. None was actually missed until the early evening, when three who were to attend a conference between an Employers' Federation and the Ministry of Works failed to appear. Others, including politicians who should have been to the House of Commons, had vanished in the same way.

None of the missing men reappeared that night.

Scotland Yard faced another influx of urgent calls which came from relatives of the missing men and from the provinces.

The middle-aged Chairman of the Midas Trust, perhaps the wealthiest single corporation in Great Britain, Lord Cardiss, left his taxi near Aldgate Station because of a traffic block, and walked to a small warehouse off the Mile End Road, where he had been ordered to meet an agent of Carosi, who would present a red disc with a specified number on it. He entered the yard hesitantly. A little man in his shirt-sleeves pointed towards an open door, and Cardiss went into the dark warehouse. Inside, rows of huge wooden barrels stood on end.

The door closed behind him, and a man came near. He felt a pain in his right arm, exclaimed aloud and said sharply: 'What's that?'

'Okay, okay,' the man said easily, and showed his red disc. 'You'll be okay.'

Cardiss lost consciousness ten minutes later, and was doubled up and pushed into one of the barrels. The lid was put on, and, with dozens of other barrels, was loaded into a lorry.

All were marked: *Fruit for Export*.

That afternoon and the following morning, a stream of barges went sluggishly down the Thames and moored alongside the small ocean-going cargo steamer at Simley's Wharf, a little up river from Tilbury. Simley's were general shipping merchants, although they specialized in fruit and flowers, which they shipped mostly to and from the Continent and Ireland. It was not a large firm, but its reputation was good.

The cargo boat, which had two stumpy funnels, a low bridge and a thick, clumsy-looking hull and stern – she looked as if she would roll badly in anything approaching a heavy sea – was dirty and smelly. The name painted on her bows was the *Snow Queen,* and she was registered at Lloyds with the rest of the small Simley fleet of coastal and ocean-going boats; they were little more than tramp-steamers.

According to the Bills of Lading, which fully satisfied the dock and customs officials, she was being loaded with a special kind of oil produced from gas – a great deal of this was shipped abroad – and the oil was in one hundred gallon barrels, as the *Snow Queen* wasn't a tanker.

No one took any special notice of the fact that some of the barrels were loaded into 'A' hold, but that most went into 'B', while some were stored on deck. There was no need to lash the deck cargo until just before the ship weighed anchor; it was due to leave on the morning tide, a little after dawn.

She carried a few passengers.

After dark on the night following the outbreak of crime, a short, stocky man, wearing a pale Homburg hat and dressed in an overcoat of American cut, strolled about the deck, accompanied by a youth who looked somewhere in his late teens. They could only just be seen from the wharf. Had there been a brighter light, anyone watching would have realised that the 'boy' was much more like a woman.

'Well, Julieta,' said Carosi, 'we have succeeded completely. We are not suspected, you see. Who is to know that *I* own Simley's and many other small wharves? No one, Julieta, except you. And who is to guess what kind of cargo we carry?'

He gave a little laugh.

'No one,' agreed Julieta. 'It is successful.'

'I promised you that. And who would guess that the barrels in "A" hold contain the men for whom the police are searching?' murmured Carosi. 'Oh, they are quite safe. They will be a little cramped, of course, but that does not matter. They will be more cramped tomorrow!' He laughed again. 'And by tomorrow, I shall tell the police I have them, and will state my price for their release.'

'Yes,' said Julieta.

'You have little to say,' complained Carosi. 'Have I not done all I promised to do?'

'I wish that the tide ran earlier,' said Julieta. 'It is a long time until dawn.'

'You need not worry,' said Carosi. 'No one will suspect us. The police have been so busy with other things. I saw to that. It is not even yet mentioned in the newspapers that these men are missing.' He pointed towards a barrel which they could just see through the gloom. 'That is marked "51". Fifty-one gentlemen are my guests. And when we are out to sea, the message will be delivered to their relations. For each of these men, and each is very wealthy, I shall require one hundred thousand pounds in gold or jewellery, delivered to good friends who have their orders and will obey. I control their whole fortunes, so they must always serve me.'

'Yes, it is a triumph,' Julieta said tonelessly.

'And although we lost Kinara and cannot send the captives there, it does not greatly matter,' said Carosi. 'We have succeeded in every way, except for Kinara. By attacking Grant and his wife, I distracted the attention of the police. Simply by the incidents at Uplands, my dear Julieta! It is always successful. One makes an attack here, and strikes somewhere else. I am almost sorry for West. The newspapers—have you seen them all, Julieta?'

'All,' said Julieta.

'That is well. I am pleased with what they say. One and all they think it has been planned by the great Carosi, and West was the policeman in charge of finding me.'

He watched her intently as he mentioned West again, but she showed no change of expression.

'And now we shall sail away, and never come back,' Carosi said. 'Aren't you pleased, Julieta? And aren't you proud—of the greatest criminal ever known? The greatest—'

'Perhaps except one,' said a little man mildly, and he appeared at their side. 'Just except one. Because no one ever suspected me, Carosi, not even Julieta! I am supposed to be just a poor wife-murderer, whereas in fact I killed her because she knew that you and I worked together. In prison I laboured long on all these plans, didn't I, Carosi? Where would you have been without me? Tell me that.'

Arthur Morely smiled into Julieta's face, and then began to laugh.

Carosi laughed, too, putting a hand on Morely's shoulder.

As they stood laughing, slow-moving barges passed close by, and two cars came on to the wharf. Then powerful lights shone out without warning, from the barges as well as the shore, and men sprang towards the cargo-boat and climbed aboard.

The crew came running, to fight.

Morely cried: 'No!' and then saw West, armed, and nearer than any of the others.

Carosi drew a gun.

West called: 'Drop it, Carosi, or—' and then two men, fighting near him, fell against him. And he lost his gun.

He saw the trio together, and knew that they could not hope to escape. He saw Morely despairing, and Carosi very still and erect, with that so-called Chinaman's smile – and with the gun in his hand.

He knew that Carosi meant to kill him. In this awful moment of failure, Carosi would want that above all else.

Then Roger saw Julieta strike Carosi's arm aside, so that he could not fire. West leapt; but before he could reach Carosi, the man had turned his gun upon the girl.

'At least we've got Carosi alive,' Chatworth said, soon afterwards. 'And Morely, too. All the captives, and all the stolen goods. Clean sweep, Roger, thank God. I'm only sorry about that girl.'

'Yes, it was hard,' Roger said, but he did not really think so.

It was far better that Julieta should be dead.

JOHN CREASEY

GIDEON'S DAY

Gideon's day is a busy one. He balances family commitments with solving a series of seemingly unrelated crimes from which a plot nonetheless evolves and a mystery is solved.

One of the most senior officers within Scotland Yard, George Gideon's crime solving abilities are in the finest traditions of London's world famous police headquarters. His analytical brain and sense of fairness is respected by colleagues and villains alike.

'The finest of all Scotland Yard series' – New York Times.

GIDEON'S FIRE

Commander George Gideon of Scotland Yard has to deal successively with news of a mass murderer, a depraved maniac, and the deaths of a family in an arson attack on an old building south of the river. This leaves little time for the crisis developing at home ....

'Gideon of Scotland Yard emerges as one of the most real working detectives in modern fiction.... A sympathetic and believable professional policeman.' - New York Times

John Creasey

The Creepers

"The prisoner's hand was thin and bony ... And in the centre of the palm was a pinkish mark. It was the shape of a wolf's head, mouth open, fangs showing. Although it was what he had expected to see, Inspector West felt a twinge of repugnance a stab not unrelated to fear. It was the fifth time he had seen the mark of the wolf – the mark of Lobo."

A gang of cat burglars led by Lobo cause mayhem as they terrorize the city. They must be stopped, but with little in the way of evidence the police are baffled. Just how can Inspector West manage to do this in what is a race against time before more victims succumb?

"Here is an excellent novel of law enforcement officers, harried, discouraged and desperately fatigued, moving inexorably ahead under the pressure of knowledge that they must succeed to save human lives." - Cleveland Plain-Dealer

"Furiously exciting" - Chicago Tribune

"The action is fast, continuous and exciting" - San Francisco News

John Creasey

The House of the Bears

Standing alone in the bleak Yorkshire Moors is Sir Rufus Marne's 'House of the Bears'. Dr. Palfrey is asked to journey there to examine an invalid - who has now disappeared. Moreover, Marne's daughter lies terribly injured after a fall from the minstrel's gallery which Dr. Palfrey discovers was no accident. He sets out to investigate and the results surprise even him . . . .

"'Palfrey' and his boys deserve to take their places among the immortals." - Western Mail

Introducing the Toff

Whilst returning home from a cricket match at his father's country home, the Honourable Richard Rollison - alias The Toff - comes across an accident which proves to be a mystery. As he delves deeper into the matter with his usual perseverance and thoroughness , murder and suspense form the backdrop to a fast moving and exciting adventure.

'The Toff has been promoted to a place of honour among amateur detectives.' – The Times Literary Supplement